A DASH OF PEACH

SWEET PEACH BAKERY #1

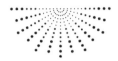

WENDY MEADOWS

MAJESTIC OWL
PUBLISHING LLC

the wallpaper reminded her of how the earth might have looked before the Great Flood of Noah. The floors were old and creaky, but Momma Peach would never hear of having them redone. She said the old floors gave character to a room and that every squeak was a voice that folks needed to listen to. Two stoves that Rosa thought were antique sat against the back wall like old friends sharing stories. A large refrigerator stood against the right wall, and old wooden cabinets held everything Momma Peach needed to bake her wonderful pies, bread, cakes and muffins. A simple kitchen sink stood on the left wall, clean as a whistle.

Rosa rested her hand on the wooden counter that ran around the entire kitchen. Everything was in perfect order, as usual. It made her feel that everything was right with the world. And of course, Momma Peach's baking table stood in the middle of the room, covered in flour as she rolled out the pie dough. A bowl of perfectly ripe peaches stood to one side, ready to be sliced.

Momma Peach nodded. "Uh, huh, I see how it is," she said and rolled her eyes with good humor. "You want the day off, don't you?"

Rosa looked down demurely. "I already called Mandy. She's agreed to cover the shift for me, Momma."

Momma Peach decided to have some fun with Rosa. She loved Rosa like the girl was her own daughter and enjoyed having fun with her. "You got a boyfriend?"

"What?" Rosa exclaimed and turned red. "No, Momma Peach... I..."

"You win the lottery and holding out on me?"

Rosa shook her head. "No, Momma Peach. I didn't win the lottery."

"You running off to the Caribbean without taking me?"

Rosa smiled as she realized Momma Peach was having fun with her. "No, Momma Peach."

"You want the day off to rub my sore shoulders?"

Rosa giggled to herself. "No, Momma Peach."

"Then tell me why you want the day off?"

Rosa drew in a deep breath and prepared to tell her, as uncomfortable as the truth was. "José, the boy I knew from my childhood, is visiting his grandparents. He's going to be in Pine Falls for two weeks. He's arriving today. Mr. and Mrs. Acosta have asked me to come over to their apartment today and see José. They're having a small welcome party."

Momma Peach grinned at Rosa. "And you want to see if little José is still the same boy you remember, is that it? Of course, it is. Tell me the truth, Rosa."

Rosa blushed again. "Well, I guess I'm a little bit curious."

Momma Peach wiped her flour-covered hands on the

white apron around her waist and walked over to Rosa. "Rosa, go see little José and satisfy your curiosity. I bet he's not so little anymore. Who knows," she said and embraced Rosa with a love that Rosa cherished with her whole heart, "maybe you might become Mrs. Acosta someday?"

"Thank you, Momma Peach," Rosa said, hugging her back as tight as she could. "You're the very best."

"No, ma'am," Momma Peach said and pointed at her table, "my peach pie is the very best, or so folks around here tell me. Now get those cute feet of yours moving, Miss Cherry Dress."

Rosa grinned and hurried out of the kitchen. Momma Peach smiled from ear to ear and began humming her song again. "Yes, how sweet the sound."

Momma Peach loved to see Rosa going out to have a good time, perhaps because she didn't have any children of her own. Her husband had died in a fatal car accident only four years after their marriage. She had started the bakery not long after and had been so busy with it she never remarried. Her parents died three months apart from each other when she was forty-three. And because she had been an only child, and her parents had come from small families too, the only relative left was her Aunt Rachel who lived in Virginia. Poor old Aunt Rachel was as forgetful as a two-year-old being told to clean her room. Some days,

Aunt Rachel was blessed to even be able to remember her name, let alone that she had a niece living down in Georgia. Momma Peach was alone in the world. But she never felt alone or thought of herself as being alone. Not when she had friends all around her. Blood didn't make folk family, she would always tell people, the heart did.

After sticking the last peach pie into the oven, Momma Peach checked the kitty-cat clock hanging over the back door. "Oh goodness," she said in a hurried voice and wiped her hands on the apron, "I better open up."

Momma Peach bustled out of the kitchen and danced out from behind the front wooden counter lined with peach cakes. The front of the bakery was a sight to see. Wooden shelves neatly displayed peach bread, peach cakes, muffins, pies, candies, brownies and other delights to fill the stomach with goodness. Wooden baskets holding fresh peaches from the small orchard out back sat against the back wall like prizes waiting to be claimed. A small cooler of bottles of homemade peach cider sat next to the baskets of peaches. The front of the bakery looked antique and old fashioned, but tended with infinite care and love, exactly like her kitchen—which was what drew the customers in. The walls were decorated with old quilt squares and baking tools, the old floors creaked while the customers waited in line, and the air always smelled of peaches and times past. The atmosphere, a customer once told her, was the secret ingredient. Momma Peach happily agreed and gave the customer a free loaf of peach bread.

"Open for business," Momma Peach said and unlocked a simple wooden door with a circular window set in it. After unlocking the front door, she turned her attention to the front display window. "No, sir," she exclaimed and perched her hands onto her hips. "No sir, not gonna have you in here today."

A single fly was buzzing around a beautiful display of peach cakes Momma Peach had baked and arranged the day before. The fly, oblivious to Momma Peach's words, continued to buzz around. Momma Peach narrowed her eyes, crept back to the front counter, and picked up the morning newspaper. "Come to Momma Peach," she whispered and slowly rolled the newspaper into a tight roll. "It's on, Mr. Fly. You and me are gonna do a little dance."

As Momma Peach eased forward toward the display window, Mandy Mayberry walked past the front display window. She stopped when she saw Momma Peach sneaking toward the window. "What in the world?" she said in a confused voice. But then she saw Momma Peach holler out loud, charge forward, and swat a newspaper roll furiously in the air. "Oh, the fly must be back," she said and giggled to herself. "Poor Momma Peach."

"Don't be afraid to meet your end, Mr. Fly, we all gotta go sometime!" Momma Peach yelled as she took one swing after another at the fly, nearly knocking over the display of peach cakes. "No, don't be afraid of ol' Momma Peach. I'll send you down the river nice and easy, sure enough."

Mandy opened the front door and watched Momma Peach swat at the fly with red cheeks and eyes that would scare a wild boar. "Good morning, Momma Peach."

"Not now, child. I'm on a mission," Momma Peach hollered and swatted at the fly again. She missed and knocked a few loaves of peach bread onto the floor in their packaging. "Pick those up for me, will you?"

Mandy closed the front door and dimpled as she watched Momma Peach. Like a soldier crawling through a battlefield being bombarded with artillery, she ducked under Momma Peach's swinging arm and scooped up the fallen loaves of peach bread, placing them back on the shelves. She stood and straightened out the soft, pale green dress she was wearing with a pair of white tennis shoes. Mandy used to get down on herself for her long skinny legs and pointed nose, until Momma Peach asked her one day, what did it hurt trying to look pretty? What did it hurt to braid her long blond hair? What did it hurt trying to feel good about herself? Nothing at all. And because Momma Peach taught her to feel proud about who she was as a twenty-year-old woman, Mandy was fiercely loyal to her. "It's over there, Momma Peach," Mandy said and pointed across the bakery. "It got away from you."

"Die!" Momma Peach yelled and charged across the bakery like a soldier exploding out of his fox hole.

"Poor fly," Mandy whispered and stashed her pink purse behind the front counter as Momma Peach continued to attack the fly.

"Where did it go?" she asked Mandy, breathing hard. "Where did the little booger get off to? Come on, Mr. Fly. Now, don't hide from me."

Mandy looked around the room but couldn't spot the fly. "I don't see the fly, Momma Peach. Maybe it—" she stopped when the front door opened and a smart but tough looking Chinese woman walked in wearing a stylish black leather jacket over a long gray dress. "Good morning, Mrs. Chan...I mean, Detective Chan."

"I wish it were a good morning," Michelle Chan said in a serious voice and looked at Momma Peach. Momma Peach was sneaking up on the far left corner of the room like a shopkeeper sneaking up on a child stealing a piece of candy. "The fly is back, I see." She suppressed a tiny smile.

"Quiet," Momma Peach fussed and threw her left hand at Michelle, "I'm about to—" Momma Peach let out a loud yell and began swatting the newspaper into the air in a flurry of useless blows.

Michelle looked at Mandy. Mandy shrugged her shoulders with a smile. "I like the way you did your hair.

You always look nice with your ponytail braided like that."

Michelle tried to smile but failed. "Thanks," she told Mandy and focused on Momma Peach.

Mandy regarded Michelle's unsmiling face. Underneath all the toughness was a kind, caring, loving woman that would lay down her life for almost anyone. On the outside, Michelle Chan was a tough cop who was an expert in several styles of martial arts but on the inside, she was a hurt woman who had lost her entire family in China before emigrating to the United States. Like Mandy, Momma Peach counted Michelle among her family.

"Momma Peach, we need to talk," Michelle said in a serious voice.

"Not now," Momma Peach exhaled.

Michelle drew in a deep breath, looked at Mandy, and then looked back at Momma Peach. "There has been a murder."

Momma Peach stopped swatting at the fly and looked at Michelle. "Mandy, go check the ovens for me."

"Yes, Momma Peach," Mandy replied and hurried away back to the kitchen.

"Talk to me." She looked at Michelle in concern.

"A man was found dead this morning," she said in a regretful voice, nodding toward the goodies surrounding her, "hunched over a plate of your peach pie."

Momma Peach stared at Michelle. Instead of becoming panicked or upset, she walked to the counter and put the newspaper down with calm hands. There was one more thing to know about her, beyond the blue striped dress and the famous peach pie. Everyone, including Michelle Chan, knew Mamma Peach was the best detective east of the Mississippi. "Who was this man? Leave nothing out for me."

Michelle reached into the right pocket of her leather jacket and pulled out a small, purple notepad and flipped it open. "Mr. Richard Lionel Graystone."

Momma Peach shook her head. "I sure don't know any Richard Graystone."

"You wouldn't," Michelle explained. "Mr. Graystone was visiting his daughter, Felicia Garland."

Momma Peach tilted her head back as she searched her memory. "Ah, the little petite thing that's married to that rich banker."

"Mr. Floyd Garland, yes," Michelle confirmed. "Momma Peach, it appears that Mr. Graystone was poisoned."

"Well, then some foul soul put poison in my pie," the older woman told Michelle in a calm and thoughtful voice. "Feel free to search my kitchens, pantry cupboards, anywhere you like. You won't find a trace of poison here. But you knew that before you even walked in my door."

Michelle nodded and leaned her right elbow onto the front counter. Before answering, she slowly drew a breath of the delightful aroma of the spices that Momma Peach used in her famous peach bread. Michelle loved the bakery and she loved Momma Peach. Momma Peach was the only real family she had left in the world. Even though she knew it would turn up very little, she had to ask her closest and dearest friend to come down to the police station for questioning. Of course, she thought, Momma Peach knew this already. "I don't know a lot about Mr. Graystone right now. I'm running a check on him as we speak. I should know more later. In the meantime—"

"I'll come down to the police station and write out a statement and answer your questions," Momma Peach told Michelle in a caring voice. "I know you have rules to follow."

Michelle sighed. "The receipt to your peach pie was found in Mr. Graystone's pants pocket, Momma Peach. The man was in your bakery yesterday."

"Maybe Rosa or Mandy sold the pie to him," Momma Peach suggested. "Mandy," she called out, "come here."

13

Michelle waited for Mandy to appear at the kitchen door. "Yes, Momma Peach?" Mandy asked in a worried voice.

"Michelle is going to describe to you a man. See if you can tell me if you recognize the man for me."

"Okay," Mandy replied in a nervous voice.

"It's okay," Momma Peach promised. "You're not in any trouble. You just ask your memory for a quick favor and we'll see what happens."

Michelle stood up to face Mandy. "Mr. Graystone, man in his mid-fifties with short, very dark red hair. He was a little overweight, but not much, and stood about 5'10" even though his driver's license claimed he was 6'2". His face," Michelle said and paused as if thinking, "well, he looked like that actor who played the dad on the sitcom Happy Days and—"

"Oh, my goodness," Mandy exclaimed, "I know who you're talking about. I wouldn't have noticed him, but that's one of my favorite classic television shows."

Momma Peach smiled proudly. "That's my baby. Now tell me about this man."

"Well," Mandy said, trying to think back, "he came in here yesterday, right before closing. Momma Peach, you were in the kitchen cleaning up and I was sweeping up front. I remember thinking that he did look like Tom Bosley, the actor who played Mr. Cunningham."

"Did this man say anything to you?" Michelle asked.

"Not really," Mandy replied and shook her head. "All he did was look around some. Wait – he did ask me if there was anything I would recommend. So I recommended Momma Peach's famous pie, of course. He paid for the pie, told me to have a nice day, and left."

Michelle looked at Momma Peach and then back at Mandy. "So Mr. Graystone came into the bakery, randomly browsed around, bought a pie, and then left?"

"Pretty much," Mandy confirmed and then added: "He did seem a little distracted."

"Distracted how?" Momma Peach pressed gently.

Mandy rubbed the tip of her nose with her right finger and then looked at the front display window. "He kept walking past the display window, kinda back and forth. At first I thought he was just browsing, but it almost looked like he was waiting to see someone walk by outside. I mean, that's how it seemed to me, anyway."

"How did Mr. Graystone pay for the pie?" Michelle asked.

"Cash," Mandy said ruefully. "I remember that because it was right after I had the money drawer counted down, too. I really wasn't expecting any more customers. I guess you live and learn."

"We all live and learn," Momma Peach reassured Mandy

and turned her attention to Michelle. "We have our work cut out for us, baby girl."

Michelle nodded. "Yes, we do."

Momma Peach looked at Mandy and was about to tell her to hold down the fort when the phone on the front counter rang. "Should I get that first?" Mandy asked. Momma Peach nodded. "Hello, Sweet Peach Bakery, this is Mandy, how can I help you? ...oh...sure, Momma Peach is right here."

"Who is it?" Momma Peach asked.

"Aunt Rachel's assisted living center."

"Oh give me strength," Momma Peach moaned and took the phone from Mandy. "This is Caroline Johnson... I see...okay...yes, put her on." Momma Peach rolled her eyes and waited. When a confused voice repeated her name, she braced herself. "Hello, Aunt Rachel, this is Caroline."

"Who?" Aunt Rachel's voice was so shrill that Mandy and Michelle could hear it plainly. Mandy suppressed a giggle, having overheard one or two of Aunt Rachel's phone calls in the past.

"Caroline...your niece," Momma Peach repeated in a loud voice. "Are you okay, Aunt Rachel?"

"Who are you?" Aunt Rachel demanded again.

Momma Peach sighed in exasperation. "It's Caroline, your niece... I'm the daughter of your brother, Ralph Johnson."

"Ralph is over at the Jenkins house playing with Roger. Now, he knows better but he don't care," Aunt Rachel told Momma Peach in a gossipy tone that made Momma Peach roll her eyes.

"Aunt Rachel," Momma Peach said, feeling her patience wearing thin and her blood pressure rising, "Ms. Halcomb said there was a problem with your monthly check. I sent your check out. Did you get it?"

"Ralph knows better than to play with Roger. Roger broke our kitchen window. Everyone knows it was Roger."

"Focus, Aunt Rachel," Momma Peach practically hollered into the phone. She could hear another voice in the background, perhaps one of the nurses.

"Who are you?" Aunt Rachel repeated in confusion.

Momma Peach closed her eyes and gently smacked the phone against her head with each word. "Aunt Rachel...pay attention!" she yelled.

"Who am I talking to? Is this you, Louise?"

"No, it's Caroline!" Momma Rachel howled and threw one hand into the air like she was testifying in church on a Sunday. "I'm going to lose it...one of these days...oh, give me strength. Aunt Rachel, please...you know your friend Louise died over ten years ago," Momma Peach finished in a patient voice. But as she watched, Mandy couldn't help but wonder if perhaps Momma Peach wouldn't rather go after Aunt Rachel one day with a rolled-up newspaper, instead of that fly.

"Louise cheats at rummy," Aunt Rachel said just as if Momma Peach hadn't said a thing. "I caught her cheating but Louise claims she wasn't. I know better."

"Why me?" Momma Peach whispered and smacked the phone against her head again. "Listen, Aunt Rachel...did you get my check or not?"

"Check? Oh yes, the nurse checks my blood pressure every morning," Aunt Rachel said proudly. "I had eggs this morning."

"Put Ms. Halcomb back on the phone," Momma Peach said through gritted teeth.

"Is this you, Louise?" Aunt Rachel asked.

"No!" Momma Peach cried out, "it's your niece Caroline!"

"Who's calling from North Carolina? Who am I speaking to?"

Momma Peach handed the phone back to Mandy. "Get Ms. Halcomb on the line for me before I go insane."

Michelle's tough demeanor finally cracked into a grin. Mandy took the phone from Momma Peach and managed to get Ms. Halcomb back on the line. "Here you go."

Momma Peach took the phone, drew in a deep breath, and closed her eyes. "Ms. Halcomb?"

"Yes."

"I'm mailing out a second check. I'm sure my first check is somewhere in my aunt's mail. But just in case the first check got lost in the mail, I'm mailing out a second check. Please see to it that the check is deposited into my aunt's account."

"Of course," Ms. Halcomb promised. "I'm sure we'll locate the first check soon, Mrs. Johnson. If we do, we'll cancel the second check and send it back to you, like last time."

"Thank you. Have a good day." Momma Peach slowly hung up the phone, leaned over the phone where it sat on the front counter, and rested her head against the wood. "Oh Lord, give me strength..."

Mandy let out a giggle and headed back into the kitchen. Even Michelle had to bite down hard on her lower lip in order not to laugh. "How is Aunt Rachel?" she finally asked.

Momma Peach stood up straight and sighed, gazing at the

phone. "She had eggs for breakfast. But that's okay because she thinks I'm Louise Jones and my Papa, rest his soul, is playing over at an old friend's house." Momma Peach turned to look at Michelle with eyes that said she was ready to quietly explode. "And it seems that she has either lost the monthly check I sent her or the check was lost in the mail. But I'm not stupid, no ma'am. I know that old bat has my check. This is the ninth time she's played this game. That old woman just loves to torment me," Momma Peach finished in a near hysterical voice and threw up her hands again. "Oh, give me strength."

Michelle gave her a sympathetic look. "Tormentors aside, are you ready to go?"

"Let me get my pocketbook," she sighed and walked back into the kitchen.

As soon as the coast was clear, Michelle let out a disbelieving laugh. She thought privately that Aunt Rachel was not nearly as senile as people assumed, but she did get bored sometimes.

CHAPTER TWO

*M*omma Peach sat patiently in front of a worn wooden desk scarred with years of police work; she counted four cigarette burns, eight coffee stains, and numerous scratches. She wondered why the police department didn't buy Michelle a new desk. "Poor baby," Momma Peach whispered, turning to look around the small, cramped office that Michelle called home when she was at the station. The office smelled of old coffee and stale donuts—she should have brought along a loaf or two of her peach bread to cover the smell. A slowly-turning ceiling fan appeared to be on its last legs, eking out a slight breeze. A wooden shelf crammed with law books was shoved up against a brown wall that needed a fresh coat of paint; the entire office needed painting, for that matter, Momma Peach thought. A tall metal filing cabinet, pockmarked with rust, huddled on the back wall to the right of the desk. It loomed over the desk like a miserable prisoner tormented by ugly nightmares; the nightmares, of course, were the case files inside filled with violent crimes. "Too much hate," Momma Peach said, shaking her head in dismay and sorrow.

A beautiful red bird landed on a flowering pink dogwood tree outside the office window. Momma Peach felt the bird land on the tree inside her heart, turned, and spotted its lustrous red feathers, and smiled. "Hello. How are you today?"

The cardinal stared through the office window at Momma Peach and then flew off and circled around the large, manicured lawn behind the police station before making its way over toward a cozy residential neighborhood. From where she was sitting, she could see the street lined with one-story ranch style homes with green yards filled with bikes, skateboards, footballs, swing sets and lawnmowers. A few kids were out in one yard tossing a football while a few other kids were climbing up into a backyard tree house. Momma Peach felt the bird's swooping flight over the neighborhood and smiled. "Fly, baby. Fly free and proud."

A few minutes later, Michelle walked into her office carrying a manila folder in her left hand and a plain donut in her right hand. "Well," she told Momma Peach in a voice that said she was back to business and prepared to work, "the check I ran on Mr. Graystone didn't turn up too much."

"Oh." Momma Peach fussed when she spotted the donut Michelle was holding, "I can't let you eat that awful thing. That little beast has ingredients in it that I can't even pronounce. Throw that ugly little creature away."

"But I'm hungry," Michelle protested. She plopped down in a rickety brown office chair that squeaked and moaned in misery. "I missed lunch."

"I will cook you a good supper tonight," she said and grabbed the big blue pocketbook sitting next to her chair. She dug through piles of odds and ends – Kleenex, Chapstick, old keys, antacids (because she didn't like her heartburn, no sir), pens, pencils, a writing pad, a change purse, a blue wallet, an old M&M toy, a few pieces of peppermint candy. "Ah," Momma Peach smiled and fished out an organic snack bar. "Here, eat this instead."

Michelle really wanted the donut. "Just a bite?" she pleaded.

Momma Peach shook her head and gave her a look. "Don't make me come across this desk."

"Yes, Momma Peach," Michelle sighed and tossed the donut into the wastebasket.

"That's my baby," Momma Peach smiled and handed

Michelle the snack bar. "Now, tell me more about Mr. Graystone."

Michelle opened the snack bar and took a bite. "Well," she said, tasting a mixture of chocolate and peanut butter, "Mr. Robert Henry Graystone, age sixty-three, came to our town from Restford, Alabama. He lived at 102 Turner Street." Michelle took another bite of the snack bar as she scanned the file in front of her. "Mr. Graystone lived alone."

"Was this man ever married? Tell me."

Michelle nodded. "Mr. Graystone was married for twenty-two years to a Nadine Florence White."

"Were they separated by death or divorce?"

"Death," Michelle explained. "Nadine White was killed by a drunk driver four years ago in Restford. I checked the records for some more info on that. The man who killed her is serving a very lengthy prison sentence, but I'm still going to check if he has any connection to Mr. Graystone or his daughter."

"Good, good," Momma Peach said with a smile. "Now read my mind and tell me what I'm thinking."

"You're wondering if Mr. Graystone had a life insurance policy," Michelle told Momma Peach as she polished off the snack bar.

Momma Peach nodded. "Tell me. Tell me."

Michelle closed the folder and handed it across the desk to Momma Peach. "They don't call you the best for nothing. Mr. Graystone had a five-hundred-thousand-dollar life insurance policy. He was also the beneficiary of a very large sum of money from his late wife's insurance policy, as well."

Momma Peach opened the folder and began scanning its contents with focused, sharp eyes. Michelle admired the brilliance that glowed in Momma Peach's beautiful eyes when she was on the trail of a mystery. "Restford is not very far from Anniston."

"About half an hour—" Michelle said and spotted a Viceroy butterfly land on the windowsill. She stared at the orange and black butterfly enviously. Far from the confines of paperwork and crime, the butterfly was free to curiously roam the world on soft wings and float on winds to new places.

Momma Peach spotted Michelle staring outside and lowered the folder in her hand. "Talk to me."

Michelle continued to gaze at the butterfly as it opened and closed its wings slowly. "Last night I went out on a date. The date...ended miserably," she said in a sad voice. "I wasn't even expecting much. I met the guy on an online dating site."

"Oh," Momma Peach admonished her, "you don't need to

search for love in a silly old computer. God gives love. Not the internet."

"I know, Momma Peach...but sometimes, I get lonely. I wanted to spend a nice evening talking to a nice man," Michelle explained. "I had him meet me down at the local coffee shop—"

"Oh, don't tell me you had a date at Wilma's," Momma Peach said indignantly. "That woman's coffee is enough to scare away my cousin Eddie. And my cousin Eddie, he can eat raw coffee grounds right out of the can."

"I know, I know," Michelle said in a chastened voice, "but the atmosphere of the coffee shop is nice and relaxing, at least. So I thought, what the heck, why not spend the evening talking to a guy who also studies martial arts and likes jazz over a cup of coffee?"

"But your fella didn't like martial arts or jazz, did he?" the older woman said softly, already reading the disappointment on Michelle's face.

Michelle shook her head no. "That Mr. Don Wilkinson didn't know the difference between Karate and Brazilian Jiu Jitsu."

"And the jazz?" Momma Peach asked in voice filled with love and not a trace of reproach for what she knew her friend would say next.

"Don heard a famous Louis Armstrong tune playing and

then told me he was really into it because he loved Nat King Cole so much," Michelle replied and then rolled her eyes. "I played along with his ignorance and pretended not to notice because I thought I could just have a nice night out. Shame on me, right, Momma Peach?"

"No," Momma Peach said. She reached across the desk and patted Michelle's hand. "I understand loneliness. Sometimes it makes us do funny things."

Michelle looked away from the butterfly and looked into Momma Peach's loving eyes. "Don left before he finished his second cup of coffee, anyway."

"He suddenly remembered that he left the iron on, right?"

"Yes," Michelle said in a miserable voice. "I don't blame the guy for getting bored. Sure, he lied to me, but to be honest, I'm about as interesting as a block of wood."

"Now don't you go believing that lie," Momma Peach gently scolded Michelle. "You're a beautiful, strong, skilled woman." Momma Peach beamed proudly at her friend. "Now, I'm not going to sit here and toot your horn, but I will say that you're my baby and you're a blessing. God loves you. And I love you."

"I love you too, Momma Peach," Michelle replied and nearly started to cry. Instead, she swallowed the lump forming in her throat and focused again on the case at hand. "So, as I was saying before...Mr. Graystone was left a lot of money by his late wife."

Momma Peach leaned back in the creaky wooden chair she was sitting in. She knew her friend had been comforted by their talk, even if Michelle was private and didn't like to share her emotions. Besides, they had other things to discuss. "Well, don't be bashful about it. I want to know how much."

"Along with his life insurance policy and the money his late wife left him, Mr. Graystone was worth one point two million. If you want the exact number, it's one million, two hundred thousand, eight hundred and forty dollars. And eight cents. That's without adding in the value of his home or vehicle and other personal belongings."

Momma Peach nodded, taking this in. "Did this poor soul have a will?"

Michelle leaned back in her chair with satisfaction. "Yes." Being a detective on a small police force was often lonely, tedious work, but working with Momma Peach made everything better. They were always on the same page.

"Where are the daughter and the husband? Leave nothing out."

"Felicia and Floyd Garland are en route to the station as we speak," Michelle explained. "We'll get to them in a minute, Momma Peach. Right now, I want to talk to you about the hotel room Mr. Graystone was found in."

"Fill my ear full."

Michelle reached out and grabbed a bottle of water sitting on the right corner of her desk. "Can I get you something to drink, Momma Peach?"

"No. I only want to drink your words. Talk to me."

Michelle took a drink of water and set the bottle back down. "Mr. Graystone was found dead at the Eagle Pine Motel out on Route 14."

Momma Peach wrinkled her nose. A foul smell entered her nostrils just hearing the name. "The Eagle Pine Motel is a blight on our fine community. The only kind of folk that dare stay at that trash heap are trash themselves." She pursed her lips. "I know my words are not Christian or kind, but they are words of truth."

"Yes, they are," Michelle agreed. "Especially when there are many other fine hotels by the interstate. The Holiday Inn Express, the Courtyard Marriott, to name a couple. Mr. Graystone had the money to stay at those hotels, too. Instead, he chose to pay $24.99 a night for a room at a rundown motel favored by drug dealers and cockroaches."

"The man was plainly in hiding," Momma Peach told Michelle. "Mandy did state, in her own opinion, that the man paced back and forth in front of the window, like he was just waiting for a living soul to walk by. Now, I can tell you that my storefront gets a lot of foot traffic. I'm sure the eyes of our murdered friend saw lots of folks walk by, too."

"I agree," Michelle told Momma Peach and rubbed her eyes, trying to concentrate. "Mr. Graystone was found dead by a housekeeper, Betty Walker."

Momma Peach looked back to the contents of the folder. "Yes, here is her statement."

"Betty Walker claims she entered Mr. Graystone's room at ten past eight this morning when nobody answered her knock. Ms. Walker stated that she was to make up the bed and bring fresh towels but then she saw him slumped over the table in the room right in front of one of your pies. At first, she thought Mr. Graystone was asleep or passed out from too much booze."

"Understandable."

"When she realized Mr. Graystone was dead, she ran from the room to get the owner," Michelle continued. "But the owner was passed out from a night of drinking. Betty said it took her about half an hour to get the man out of bed."

"Leaving the body in the open for half an hour," Momma Peach pointed out.

"Yes."

Momma Peach nodded and continued to examine the contents of the folder. "I want to see the motel room."

"Yes, ma'am, as soon as we can."

"I know Mr. Graystone wasn't eating my peach pie and watching television when he died. I know you know that, too," Momma Peach told Michelle with a look from under her furrowed brow. "Someone else must have been involved."

"Momma Peach, I examined the motel room," Michelle explained. "I went through Mr. Graystone's suitcase and wallet. I picked through the bathroom. I went through his car. Mr. Graystone was clean. I didn't find anything except the normal stuff...clothes, deodorant, toothpaste, cologne, a car map, some gum, nothing out of the ordinary. The motel room was a dump, sure, but it was clean of any evidence of a crime...as far as I could see. No sign of forced entry or violence. So...nobody broke in and forced him to eat a poisoned pie. Right now, as it stands, we have absolutely nothing to go on. I'll show you the motel room, but I don't think you'll find anything. That's why I wanted to talk to you first."

Momma Peach nodded her head. "You let me worry about the motel room. Now, tell me what kind of wheels did Mr. Graystone have under his backside?"

"A classic 1979 Volvo 265, one of those beautiful old

station wagons, green in color...with, if I remember right...close to two hundred thousand miles. I did find a receipt in the glove compartment for a recent oil change."

"When?"

"Monday of last week, on the 22nd," Michelle stated. "The deceased rented the motel room on the 24th and was pronounced dead on the 29th."

"Mr. Graystone was found dead on early Monday morning," Momma Peach corrected Michelle. "Let's not become cold-hearted toward the dead."

Michelle nodded. She respected Momma Peach's personal approach to each homicide case. Deep down in her own heart, she wished she had Momma Peach's compassion for people. On each homicide case, she had to harden her heart even more just to get through her work in one piece, and on her worst days, she considered even the victims no better than criminals. Thankfully, she had her friend, mentor, and the best amateur detective south of the Mason Dixon line to remind her what was truly important. "Yes, Momma Peach."

"When a poor soul is murdered and taken away from the earth earlier than expected, we must show respect. Please don't think I'm scolding you."

"I know, Momma Peach," Michelle promised.

"Now," Momma Peach said, "we know Mr. Graystone,

the poor soul, was in town from the 24th until he was found dead this morning. So, what was he doing in town? Did he talk to his daughter?"

Michelle shook her head. "Felicia Garland sounded shocked when I told her about her father being in town. She claimed she hadn't heard from her father in years due to a personal disagreement."

"You talked to Felicia personally?"

Michelle nodded. "She's next of kin so I had to notify her, and she'll have to identify the body. Before I went to see you, I stopped by her home on Maple Lane to tell her the bad news."

Momma Peach looked impressed but wary. "Maple Lane is a very fancy neighborhood. Lots and lots of money there...lots and lots of money."

"Tell me about it," Michelle replied. "The home Felicia Garland and her husband own costs more money than I could ever earn working as a homicide detective. Especially an underpaid one."

"Well, honor and money do not play well together," Momma Peach warned. "There may be more to Felicia than we know. Right now, tell me how Little Miss Fancy Britches reacted when you told her about the death of her father?"

"Fake tears, plastic emotions...same old, same old,"

Michelle told Momma Peach. "I mean, let's face it, Felicia Garland isn't known for donating her time to soup kitchens."

"Now, I don't know Felicia too well. I only saw her at the big First Baptist Church downtown a few times for a special sermon from a visiting preacher man."

Guilt struck Michelle's heart. She hadn't stepped foot in a church in years. "You'll get to know Felicia better today," she promised Momma Peach.

Momma Peach shook her head. "No. I don't want anyone knowing that I'm working this case. The interrogation room has a one-way window. I will stand in the viewing room and watch you talk to Felicia and her husband."

"Are you sure, Momma Peach?"

Momma Peach nodded as she worked on the piece of candy in her mouth, her mind and eyes locked on the folder she was holding. "I have Mandy and Rosa to think about. Supposing Felicia Garland has absolutely nothing to do with murdering her father, but she might try and cause damage to my bakery and the people I love, out of revenge."

"Because Mr. Garland died eating your famous peach pie?"

"Yes," Momma Peach assured Michelle, "and other reasons that I won't explain right now."

"I didn't tell Felicia how her father died."

"Don't matter. In this town, people have ways of pulling splinters out of the tiger's eye," Momma Peach promised.

Michelle began to speak but the phone on her desk rang. Michelle grabbed it before the first ring had finished. "Yes? Okay, take them to the interrogation room. I'll be there in a few minutes." Michelle put down the phone. "They're here."

Momma Peach closed the folder. She began to stand up when her ears caught the sound of a fly. "Oh, no you didn't," she said in a voice that told Michelle a war was coming. Momma Peach slowly stood up and searched the office. "Ah," she said, spotting a fly buzzing around the bottom of the window, "I see you...now just stay very still..."

Michelle watched Momma Peach try to roll up the folder in her hand. She started. "Not the case file, Momma Peach!" Momma Peach looked at her in surprise and flattened out the file. "We don't have time for this, anyway," she said good-naturedly.

"Oh, I will be back for you," Momma Peach whispered to the fly at the window. She swung her purse toward it.

The fly spotted Momma Peach at the last possible second and took flight as if it knew what the woman with the huge blue purse was up to. Momma Peach let out an outraged groan as she followed Michelle to the interrogation room.

Felicia Garland walked into a small room with gray walls that held a plain metal table with two chairs on opposite sides. She noted a mirror on the east wall that was undoubtedly a one-way observation window. "Am I being arrested?" she asked the short, plump cop who looked like he knew more about donuts than criminal procedure.

"No, ma'am," the cop told Felicia, clearly admiring her overpowering beauty. "Detective Chan just wants to ask you a few questions."

"Very well," Felicia said in an annoyed tone, holding her head high like the high school beauty queen she had once been. Now thirty-five, her long, blond hair still tumbled below her shoulders in perfect waves. Her brilliant blue eyes were flirty when she wanted them to be. Her beauty was powerful enough to force any man to his knees. Or so Felicia thought. In reality, her beauty was washed out and her pink suit looked more like a melted marshmallow than the chic outfit she probably believed it to be—at least that's what Momma Peach thought as she sat down in a wooden chair behind the one-way window in a stuffy viewing room that smelled of stale coffee.

Felicia planted herself in one of the metal chairs and

waited for Michelle. She placed her expensive white leather purse down into the metal gray table, opened it, and fished out an orange mint. Michelle entered the room a couple of minutes later, carrying two bottles of cold water. "I thought Mr. Garland was with you?" she asked Felicia without saying hello.

"My husband had urgent business at the bank," Felicia answered impatiently. "Honestly, detective, didn't I answer all of your questions earlier?"

"I'm sorry, but no," Michelle said, setting the two bottles of water down on the table. "Water?"

"No, thank you."

"I'll need to speak to Mr. Garland," Michelle said to Felicia as she pulled out her metal chair and sat down. "Your father has been found dead, Mrs. Garland. My sincere condolences, again, for your tragic loss. But this is serious business. I understand your husband is a very busy man, but he needs to make time to talk with me. I want him down here at the station no later than noon tomorrow."

Michelle's demand did not please Felicia one bit. Momma Peach watched Felicia's expression turn annoyed and dismissive. "I'm sure my husband will come by to speak with you when he has the time."

"No, ma'am," Michelle corrected Felicia in a voice like a teacher who wasn't going to put up with a smart-mouthed student. "I want Mr. Garland down here by noon tomorrow unless he wants me to show up to fetch him in front of all his bank customers, is that clear?"

Felicia avoided Michelle's eyes, looking down at her soft, manicured hands. "I will speak to my husband and tell him that you need to speak to him by noon tomorrow. It's up to him if he will come or not."

"If he refuses to speak to me I will get a warrant," Michelle promised. "Now, Mrs. Garland, the reason I asked you here is because I need to ask you a series of questions."

Felicia finally raised her eyes and looked Michelle in the face. She knew Michelle Chan wasn't just some sap off the street. Felicia saw a skilled detective sitting before her; a detective known for her mind as much as for her fighting skills. The last physical fight Felicia had been in was back in her junior year of high school when she tangled with Noelle Myers for flirting with her boyfriend. Unfortunately, Noelle Myers had wiped the floor of the girl's locker room with Felicia. After that fight, Felicia swore to never lose again, and so had learned to use different tactics to defeat her enemies. "I already told you what I know. I was never close to my family. I told you that my father and I haven't spoken since my mother was killed by a drunk driver."

Momma Peach observed Felicia's face carefully through the one-way glass. Most curious and heart-breaking was the fact that the girl showed no sadness at the mention of her own mother's death. It made Momma Peach wonder.

"Why is it that you were estranged?" Michelle asked and picked up a bottle of water.

Felicia watched Michelle open the bottle of water in her hand with careful eyes. "My mother and I were never exactly...close," Felicia said. "My mother was very conservative in her views, as was her side of the family. As a teenager, I couldn't move an inch without her scolding me for this or that, usually for something stupid like coming in an hour past my curfew or getting low marks on my report cards. In her eyes, I had to be absolutely perfect. It wasn't my fault I failed chemistry." Felicia rolled her eyes at this last part.

"And her attitude made you rebel, was that it?"

Felicia shrugged her shoulders. "You were a teenage girl once. Sometimes you see your parents as the enemy. You know how it is."

"My parents were murdered when I was sixteen years old," Michelle informed Felicia in an even tone. "They were murdered for standing up for the rights of innocent people. I didn't have a chance to be a teenager. I was too busy running for my life."

Felicia was at a loss for words. Michelle's look told her wordlessly to knock off the pity party and act like an adult. There was an awkward silence before Felicia continued. "Well...my mother and I had different views, detective."

"And your father, Mr. Graystone, did you have different views from him, as well?"

Momma Peach leaned forward in her seat and studied Felicia's face with her keen eyes through the mirror. "My father shared my mother's views, yes. He never once played referee. I was always getting penalized by a very cruel woman who didn't care about my feelings, my views, or my thoughts." Her voice was petulant but with an undercurrent of barely-suppressed anger. "But," Felicia continued, forcing her tone to become more neutral, "after I graduated high school and left home, my father and I managed to talk a few times on the phone. We never became close, but he seemed to cool down...some. He even managed to convince me to come back home and see my mother a handful of times."

"Did you?"

"Sure," Felicia said, "she was my mother, after all. But after she was killed, my father changed. He became bitter. It was impossible to talk to him...so I stopped. What was the point in trying to talk to a man who blamed everyone but himself for my mother's death?"

"What do you mean?"

"My mother was half blind," Felicia said in a resentful voice that Momma Peach didn't like. "Sure, she was hit by a drunk driver, but sometimes I wonder...was it just bad luck or did my mother run that red light because she didn't see it? I guess I'll never know. But what I do know is that my mother should have never been allowed behind the wheel of a car that late at night. My father knew she was half blind...what was he thinking?"

Michelle didn't comment, watching Felicia's face go from angry back to neutral again. She changed direction. "Did Mr. Graystone have a will?"

Momma Peach watched Felicia's spine stiffen. Evidently the pain of this was still fresh, despite all her nonsense about an estrangement. "Yes, he did. But don't think for a second that he left me a dime. After my mother died, my father changed his will, or so he told me in the midst of one of our last arguments. He said he was leaving everything he had to the local veterans group in Restford."

"Mr. Graystone was a veteran?"

Felicia nodded her head. "He served in the Army during Vietnam," she said. "My father never spoke about his time in the Army, though. All I knew growing up was that he flew helicopters."

"He was a pilot?"

"In his younger days, maybe, though you wouldn't have known it," Felicia huffed. "All my father did while I was growing up was fix toilets and unclog sinks."

"So he was a plumber."

"Yes," Felicia confirmed in a disgusted tone. "What my mother saw in my father I'll never know."

Michelle glanced discreetly at the one-way mirror, knowing this display of lack of respect would probably cause some choice words to come out of Momma Peach's mouth. "Your mother left your father a large sum of money when she died. What did she do for a living?"

Michelle could see that her question took the wind out of Felicia. A look of worry crossed her face and she smoothed back her blonde hair in an attempt to cover her reaction. "My mother's side of the family were all lawyers. She inherited some money but also practiced law for a number of years before she married my father."

"Okay," Michelle said and took a long sip of water as if she had not noticed Felicia's slip at all. "Mrs. Garland, do you have any idea why your father was in town?"

"How should I know?" Felicia said defensively.

Michelle nodded her head. "Did you have any reason to kill your father?"

"What?!" Felicia cried out in outrage. She stormed to her feet. "I don't have to sit here and—"

"Sit," Michelle said in a tone that made Felicia close her mouth and sit back down in her seat. "These are routine questions, Mrs. Garland. I have to ask them." She gazed at Felicia with a neutral expression as if stunned that she would even take offense.

Felicia folded her arms. "The questions you're asking me are simply stupid and insulting."

"Maybe," Michelle said, remaining calm. "Mrs. Garland, I'll ask you again. Did you have any reason to kill your father?"

"Sure," Felicia said, perhaps hoping her sarcasm would appear fierce even though Michelle clearly intimidated her, "I killed my father because he left all of his money to a bunch of wrinkly old men who sit around playing checkers all day and telling worn-out war stories."

"I want a direct answer, Mrs. Garland."

"No," Felicia nearly screamed, "I didn't have any reason to kill my father. I don't even know why he was in town, for crying out loud."

Behind the window, Momma Peach shook her head. "Liar," she whispered. She enjoyed how Michelle's technique had drawn out such answers from Felicia Garland. Where there was smoke, there was bound to be the devil's fire.

"Did your father have any enemies?" Michelle asked.

"How should I know?"

"I wonder if perhaps Mr. Graystone might have come

43

here seeking your help," Michelle stated in a mild tone. Momma Peach smiled and gave out a low chuckle around the candy she was still sucking on.

Felicia stared into Michelle's eyes. And then, she changed her tone. "I guess that's a possibility. I'm not sure. I mean, most people liked my father. He wasn't a bad person or anything. He got along well with most everyone he met. But...I guess anyone can make enemies."

"Did your father have any problems with drugs, alcohol...any gambling?" Michelle asked, draining the bottle of water in her hand. She could tell Felicia was pleased at the opportunity to cast suspicion onto anyone and anything else at hand.

Felicia drew in a deep breath and let out a dramatic sigh. "How should I know, Detective Chan? I told you we weren't that close. And frankly, this has been a very exhausting morning for me. I had to go down to the morgue at the hospital and identify my father's body and then sign one paper after the next. I can't even begin planning for his funeral until the state returns his body from the crime lab."

"Your father was poisoned."

"How do you know that?"

Michelle carefully clasped her hands together. "That's not a detail the police department is authorized to share at this time, sadly. But I can share that I know Mr. Graystone was poisoned. And that we don't know who poisoned your father."

"A very sick and disturbed person, obviously," Felicia said quickly, in a nasty voice, and then added: "By the way, Detective Chan, you never told me where my father's body was found. May I please know?"

"No," Michelle said, "you may not. My apologies. If your father's murder is due to involvement with drugs, gambling, a grudge, or some other reason, then the person who killed your father may still be lurking around town. Your life could be in danger, too, in fact."

Momma Peach smiled again. Michelle was a pro. "I understand," Felicia said in a falsely worried voice. "So, you think the person who killed my father may come after me?" she asked.

"It's possible."

"Oh, dear," Felicia said. "Maybe I should call my husband and have him come down here immediately."

"Tomorrow before noon will be fine," Michelle told Felicia as she suppressed a smirk at this sudden change in Mr. Garland's availability. She snuck another glance at the one-way mirror. "Mrs. Garland, I need you to stay in town. Don't leave. An officer will be watching your home, just in case."

"I understand." Michelle could see a tiny muscle in Felicia's neck twitch at that. She thought she had escaped suspicion – she wasn't expecting surveillance.

"I also need you to write down the names of anyone you know who associated with your father. Relatives, friends, co-workers, old Army pals, anybody. Okay?"

"Sure."

"I need names, addresses, phone numbers, anything you can come up with. I know you were estranged, but you are our best source of information right now," Michelle explained. "We're reaching out to his Army buddies, but from my initial call it doesn't sound like he actually spent much time with the veteran's group."

"I'll do my best," Felicia promised.

Michelle stood up. "I think I have all I need from you for now. We'll speak more tomorrow when your husband comes down to the station."

"I'm free to leave?"

"Of course," said Michelle with a look of innocent surprise. "You were never under arrest, of course. After you write out your statement and the names of anyone who was associated with your father, you can leave. But stay in town. If you leave, that'll make my superiors think you did have something to do with your father's murder. As it stands right now, I think you're in the clear."

"I didn't kill my father, Detective Chan," Felicia said in a voice filled with petty disdain.

"Let's do our best to make sure you fill out the paperwork so we can prove it," Michelle said, and walked out of the interrogation room. Momma Peach remained in the viewing room. She watched Felicia glance at the one-way mirror and shake her head in frustration. "Okay, little girl," Momma Peach said and rose to her feet, "I know who you are now and I am going to play your twisted little game."

Momma Peach walked out of the viewing room and met Michelle in the hallway. "Well?" Michelle asked.

"I have a lot of thoughts walking back and forth in my mind," Momma Peach told Michelle in a solemn voice.

"Did Felicia Garland kill her father?" Michelle asked.

Momma Peach glanced up and down a long, gray, brick hallway. The hallway was clear. "I think more than one person killed Mr. Graystone, the poor soul. I think Felicia Garland is a hideous black widow spider married to a deadly scorpion."

"I was thinking something along that line," Michelle said and leaned back against the wall. "Momma Peach, even if you get past her awful attitude, there's a sour smell coming from Felicia Garland that made me want to kick her right in the face. It took everything in me to control my temper."

"You did good," Momma Peach promised Michelle. "I saw the warrior in your eyes desperately wanting to pull out her sword and issue justice. And justice will be served soon, and with a large spoon."

Michelle nodded. "Want to go to the motel now?"

"Yes," Momma Peach said, "but first, I want to ask you a few questions."

"Okay."

Momma Peach took Michelle's left hand and walked her outside into a side parking lot. A soft, warm, gentle breeze was blowing. Momma Peach took a few seconds and soaked in the breeze with grateful eyes. She breathed in the afternoon air with love and gratefulness. "The Good Lord sure knows how to make the air sweet."

The heavy scent of dogwood and magnolia trees played in the air, mingled with a dash of honeysuckle and roses. Michelle looked up through the branches of a large mighty pine tree and spotted a soft, blue sky shimmering through the branches like a faraway lake dancing in the bright sun. "Lovely day to take a picnic down by the lake."

"Yes, it is," Momma Peach agreed. "But I can't pack us a picnic right now."

Michelle nodded and looked into Momma Peach's

thoughtful face. "What questions did you want to ask me, Momma Peach?"

"Michelle," Momma Peach said, "is it possible, in your own mind, that Felicia Garland and her husband hired a killer to poison Mr. Graystone? That poor, poor, soul."

"Maybe," Michelle answered. "I don't think those two are the kind of people who like to get their hands dirty."

"I felt that in my heart, too," Momma Peach admitted. "We have a lot of folks in the kitchen right now that need to be sorted out. I want to sort each person out one at a time in order not to get her mind confused. My, but Aunt Rachel confused my mind enough already this morning...oh, give me the strength to deal with that woman...give me the strength."

Michelle grinned. "Momma Peach, do you really think Aunt Rachel loses your checks on purpose?"

Momma Peach narrowed her eyes and hunched her shoulders in distaste. "That woman is torture some days...torture, I tell you. I know she lays awake at night thinking of ways to torment my mind. I can feel her lying awake, staring at my photo, smiling to herself."

Michelle let out a quick laugh. "Aunt Rachel is an old lady, Momma Peach. Surely she isn't as evil as you think."

Momma Peach nodded. "I know the devil's handiwork when I see it. Aunt Rachel has too much idle time on her hands in that rest home, and I pray she finds something better to do than call my bakery whenever she wants to stir the pot. Now, let me ask you one last question and then we'll go."

"Fire away."

"I want to know what you found in Mr. Graystone's wallet. Did you find a bank card?"

Michelle shook her head no. "No, Momma Peach. I found Mr. Graystone's driver's license, social security card, some photos of his wife, and over eight hundred dollars in cash. I didn't find a bank card."

Momma Peach nodded. "And Mr. Graystone paid for my peach pie with cash, too."

"Momma Peach, what are you getting at?" Michelle asked.

Momma Peach rubbed her chin with her left hand. Holding her blue pocketbook looped over her right shoulder was a real chore, but a proper woman, Momma Peach told her babies, never left home without carrying her pocketbook. Of course, Momma Peach knew, there were times when stuffing a simple wallet down her bosom seemed tempting. Men had it easy. Women had to carry everything and the darn kitchen sink around in their pocketbook.

"Michelle," Momma Peach told Michelle, "I bet you ten

of my peach pies that Mr. Graystone closed down his bank account long ago and that all of his money isn't where Felicia Garland thinks it is. No ma'am," Momma Peach said in a confident voice, "I know what kind of woman Felicia Garland is. I saw her eyes. I looked into her heart."

Michelle stared at Momma Peach, curious about this potential line of investigation. "I'll run a check and see, Momma Peach."

"After I examine the motel room," Momma Peach told Michelle and patted her hand. "Now, take me to the motel and afterward help her cleanse her body with bleach and rubbing alcohol. Oh, give me the strength...give me the strength to enter the den of sin that is the Pine Eagle Motel."

CHAPTER THREE

*M*omma Peach watched a gruff-looking character with long, stringy gray hair open the dirty motel room door with a key dangling from a ring of half-rusted keys. "I don't like cigarettes," she said, waving away the thick smoke rising from a cigarette the man held in the corner of his mouth.

The man shrugged his shoulders, popped open the door, and looked at Momma Peach with his gray eyes. "Not my problem. Lock the door on your way out," he said in an irritated voice.

"Show some manners," Momma Peach said with a scowl and smacked the man in the head with her pocketbook. "I don't tolerate no rudeness, Mr. Thompson."

Michelle watched Mark Thompson stumble backward and nearly trip over his own skinny legs. He managed to catch his balance before backing up into the filthy parking lot. "What's with you, lady!?" he yelled and began rubbing the right side of his face with his left hand without realizing that the cigarette in his mouth was now crushed.

Momma Peach wound up her pocketbook and prepared to launch a second attack. "Watch how you speak to your betters. You say you run this place but you smell like a wet rat," she growled, "I don't like wet rats. And look at your shirt. Is that a white t-shirt or a yellow one?" Momma Peach swung her pocketbook in Mark's direction with a menacing look. Mark ran further into the dirty parking lot and hid behind a tan 1988 Oldsmobile. "You're crazy!" he shouted. "Arrest her," he tried to order Michelle.

"I have real work to do," Michelle told Mark in a cold tone. "Don't you?"

Momma Peach watched Michelle ease her way under the yellow crime scene tape and into the motel room where Mr. Graystone had been found dead. "Go wash your face and brush your teeth," she told Mark in a voice that would have made a herd of lions run scared. "I try to see the best in people, the way Jesus teaches me to. Jesus never said we had to live this life dirty and smelling like a rat. Somewhere there has to be some good in you."

Mark finally took the hint and hurried away toward the

run-down green building that served as the motel's front office.

Momma Peach sighed. "Going back to the bottle, no doubt," she said in a sad voice. "Well, I have work to do."

Momma Peach walked under the yellow tape and through the door, entering a dimly lit, smelly room covered with ugly green carpet and even uglier green walls. Two queen beds stood in the room like twin dead brains, each covered with a blanket in a disgusting hue of decaying pinkish-brown. The color of the blankets against the hideous green of the walls made for a terrible contrast. A flimsy, chipped table equipped with two rickety wooden chairs was shoved up against the back wall, near a rusted sink. Momma Peach didn't see a television set or night stand. "I love the color green," she told Michelle, "because green covers the earth. But this green...no sir, I don't like this green at all."

"It is ugly," Michelle agreed and closed the door. She looked around with dismay. "Momma Peach, someone has been in this room. Smell the smoke?"

Momma Peach sniffed the air. "Cigar smoke."

Michelle nodded. "Smell the cologne, too?"

Momma Peach nodded. "Yes, I smell it. I also smell a second cologne." Momma Peach walked to the flimsy wooden table, bent down, and sniffed one of the wooden chairs sitting at the table. Then she moved to the second wooden chair and sniffed it. "Mr. Graystone, rest his soul, was sitting in that chair," Momma Peach said and pointed to the first wooden chair.

"Yes, he was," Michelle confirmed, impressed as always by Momma Peach's quick work and unerring sense of smell.

"He was wearing a very nice cologne that I like," Momma Peach added. "But the other cologne infesting this room smells like money."

"I agree," Michelle told Momma Peach. They each privately wondered about the second cologne. It clearly hadn't come from the motel's proprietor. The room had been cleared to be cleaned under supervision, but after that, any police officer's visit would have been logged, and they had checked the log before their visit. Who had been in the room?

Momma Peach grew silent. Slowly and methodically she began to explore every aspect of the ugly room. Michelle leaned back against the door and watched. "Take notes." Michelle nodded her head and pulled a small writing pad out from the inside pocket of her black leather jacket. "Carpet has been vacuumed...both beds have been made...table has been wiped down with furniture polish..." Momma Peach braced herself and entered the bathroom. "Oh, give me strength," she cried as her eyes took in a filthy toilet, a gray tub ringed with soap scum, a green tiled floor splattered with grime and who knows what varieties of contagious diseases. To cap it all off, a roll of cheap toilet paper sat askew on the toilet lid. She backed out of the bathroom as if someone had hit her in the head with a baseball bat and slammed the door shut. "Scald me down with bleach!" she yelled.

"Yeah, it's pretty bad in there," Michelle said wryly.

Momma Peach backed further away from the bathroom door, staring at it like it was the devil incarnate. "This room has been cleaned...bathroom untouched...write that down."

Michelle made the note. "Momma Peach, someone came back searching for something, didn't they?"

"Yes, I want to talk to Betty."

"Me, too," Michelle agreed and yanked the door open. "I've had enough, have you? Let's get out of here."

"Me first," Momma Peach said and ran out into the bright sunlight. She hurried over to the hood of the Oldsmobile, yanked open her pocketbook, and withdrew a bottle of rubbing alcohol. "Come to Momma Peach," Momma Peach said and began pouring the rubbing alcohol all over her hands, arms, and face and then focused on Michelle. "Come here."

Michelle knew better than to argue, having worked with Momma Peach on cases before. She walked over to Momma Peach with a sense of dread. Momma Peach began dousing her hands with the rubbing alcohol as Michelle tried in vain to hold her breath. Momma Peach went to work on Michelle's face like she was a small child who needed a spit bath. "I can't...breathe," Michelle said and began coughing. "Fumes...really strong, Momma Peach...can't breathe..."

"Cleanses the lungs," Momma Peach said with satisfaction, inspecting Michelle's face. "I know about germs. Germs just don't sit on the hands. Those nasty little critters are everywhere."

"Yes, Momma Peach," Michelle said and turned her head to the side to gulp in a few deep breaths of air.

Momma Peach finally smiled, put the bottle of rubbing alcohol back in her pocketbook, and threw a disparaging glance at the front office. The motel was surrounded by tall pine trees and raggedy patches of tall grass that hadn't seen a lawn mower in decades, or so it seemed. "This place is a wart on the backside of our lovely town."

"Oh, well..." Michelle stopped to examine the depressing exterior of the motel, "there's a few more warts in our town, Momma Peach, besides this place."

"I know there are," Momma Peach replied and shook her head. "These days I think that most folks don't care what their town looks like in the far corners just as long as they get to sit and sip tea in the pretty places. I remember visiting the old trailer park out on the old farm road."

"Didn't the town council condemn that trailer park?"

Momma Peach nodded. "But not soon enough," she said in a sad voice. "I used to take food to the children living in that awful place. "What I saw still haunts my dreams today. For the first time in my life, I was grateful to see the Department of Family and Children Services step in. They had to come and remove children from people who cared more about beer than they did about a sweet six-month-old baby sitting in his own dirty diaper for days at a time."

"How awful."

"I'm grateful that some of the babies I saw in that trailer park are now in college preparing for their own families," Momma Peach told Michelle. "Go fetch Betty. I'll stand here beside your car and think some."

"Okay," Michelle agreed and walked off toward the front office. Momma Peach smiled. "That's my baby."

As Momma Peach waited for Michelle to return with Betty, she let her mind wander around a certain question that was buzzing inside of her mind like an early spring bee. "Now where have I smelled that cologne before?" she asked herself. "At the grocery store? Nah. Mr. Bosley doesn't wear money cologne. Maybe at the post office?" Momma Peach wrinkled her nose. "Nah. Mr. Griffin is too grumpy to wear money cologne. Maybe...at church?" Momma Peach shook her head. "Ain't no soul in my church rich enough to wear money," she chuckled to herself. "Pastor Duncan barely has enough money to buy socks without holes in them, bless his soul."

A few minutes later Michelle walked out of the front office empty handed. She returned to Momma Peach with a frustrated look in her eyes. "Betty quit," she told Momma Peach. "And that stubborn mule inside is too busy drinking to care about performing his civic duty to help us."

"Did you tell Mr. Smelly-Breath you could come back with a warrant?"

"Yeah," Michelle said with a huff. "But from his response, I don't think we'd get a thing. It's not likely he has legal employment records because he probably pays under the table."

"Didn't you get Betty's personal information from her earlier?"

"I did," Michelle explained, "but Momma Peach, I don't think the woman gave me factual information." Michelle cast a furious glance at the front office. "Betty was very nervous when I questioned her. She looked like a street drunk herself who was sober just long enough to earn her next bottle of liquor."

"I know her kind," Momma Peach told Michelle. She closed her eyes and began thinking. "Mr. Smelly-Breath in there needs another good slap upside the head with my pocketbook."

"He's getting too liquored up to care," Michelle explained. "He will, though," she promised. "I'm going to shut this rat-trap down once and for all."

"In time," Momma Peach told Michelle, her eyes still closed in thought. Suddenly, her eyes flew open in alarm. "First, we have to check the bus station. Drive fast and forget your car has a brake." Momma Peach said in a quick voice and hurried around to get in on the passenger side of the Oldsmobile.

Michelle, realizing Momma Peach's exact line of thinking, dove quickly into the driver's seat. "Hold on Momma Peach!" The Oldsmobile jerked backward as she slammed it into gear and sped out of the dirty parking lot. They left behind black skid marks as a present.

"I'm a-holding on," Momma Peach yelled back and braced her hands against the dashboard. "Oh, don't send me to Heaven early."

Michelle leaned forward to grip the steering wheel. "You told me to forget this car has a brake," Michelle grinned as she sped down a road lined with tall pine trees, their branches like green hands stretching up into the blue sky.

"I might have spoken foolishly," Momma Peach cried out as Michelle raced the Oldsmobile around a slow-moving truck. The old man in the driver's seat turned to look at them as the Oldsmobile raced by. Momma Peach smiled and offered a nervous wave. The old man shook his head and turned back to the wheel. "Oh, give me strength," she begged in an undertone.

Michelle pressed down harder on the gas pedal. "Hold on, Momma Peach!"

"Oh goodness," Momma Peach cried, "I want to meet the angels, but not now!"

"The three o'clock bus leaves town in less than ten minutes. If Betty Walker is trying to skip town, then we have to beat the bus."

Momma Peach closed her eyes. "I think someone paid Betty to leave town," she said over the roar of the engine, reaching out for calm thoughts like butterflies to soothe her scared mind. But instead of butterflies, a swarm of annoying flies buzzed around her head. "Shoo, get out of my mind," she ordered the flies.

Momma Peach cracked open one eye, spotted Michelle racing up behind a slow-moving tractor, and slammed her eye shut with a strangled half-scream. The car swayed as Michelle raced around the tractor at the last second. "Ebenezer Scrooge didn't need to see his past, present, and future to straighten out his heart...all he needed was one car ride with you."

Michelle kept her right foot pressed down on the gas

pedal. "Momma Peach, do you think Floyd Garland paid Betty Walker to leave town?"

"Maybe," Momma Peach inched her right eye open a tad and peeked around. "Still alive. Oh, thank you!"

"It's possible Betty won't be at the bus station," Michelle pointed out, though she didn't slow the car down for one second. "If Floyd Garland paid her to take a hike he might have sent her out of town by a different route."

"I know that. But I know that some folk are very narrow-minded in this town. I think a high-falutin man like our Mr. Garland would sooner give Betty a ticket and then wash his hands of the whole thing. So we have to take a peek at the bus station and...oh, give me strength!" Momma Peach cried out again as Michelle raced past a gray Toyota.

Michelle focused on her driving while her mind whirled around her thoughts. "The coroner will tell us what kind of poison killed Mr. Graystone. That'll be a good lead."

"Yes," Momma Peach said taking deep breaths. "Baby...do you love me?"

"Of course."

Momma Peach grabbed Michelle's right arm with her left hand. "Then slow down."

Michelle glanced at Momma Peach's frightened face. She eased off the gas a little. "Better?"

"Next time I tell you to drive fast...slap me."

Michelle grinned. "Okay, Momma Peach," she said and maintained a steady speed. When she pulled the car up to the small brick building of the bus depot, she spotted the Greyhound bus still idling in the parking lot. Michelle jumped out of the Oldsmobile and jogged up to the door of the bus and looked up at the gentle face of a black driver sitting behind the wheel. "Any passengers yet?" she asked and displayed her badge.

"Not yet," the driver replied to Michelle. "I just pulled in about five minutes ago."

Michelle walked up the steps and looked down the long aisle of the Greyhound bus. She counted fourteen faces. Seven women, five men, and two children. Betty was absent among the faces. Still, Michelle thought, as she hurried down the aisle to check the bathroom, you could never be too careful. "Anyone in there?" Michelle asked and knocked on the bathroom door. A ten-year-old boy stepped out of the bathroom, looked up at Michelle with curious eyes and said "Wait your turn, lady."

Michelle smiled. "Sure, kid," she said and walked back to the front of the bus. Three children, she amended the count in her head. "Nobody gets off, okay," she told the driver.

"I understand," the driver told Michelle and leaned back in his seat. "Anything I should be worried about?"

"I'm looking for a certain woman," Michelle said and gave Betty's description to the driver. "This bus is heading toward Orlando, right?"

"Yes, ma'am."

"Okay," Michelle told the driver and walked down the front steps. "I know how many people are on this bus. I'll do a second count when you leave. I'm going inside to search the depot. If anyone tries to get on that matches that description I gave you, please let her on the bus but don't leave until I come back."

"Yes, ma'am," the driver promised Michelle.

Michelle spotted Momma Peach walking through the front door of the brick building. She jogged over to her and nodded at the bus. "The bus is clear."

Momma Peach smiled. "Good," she said, stepping into the cool lobby. A single wooden bench sat in the middle of the lobby facing a ticket counter, and a light brown carpet covered the floor. Two bathrooms stood at the back of the lobby, separated by a drinking fountain and a soda and snack machine. Betty was nowhere in sight. Momma Peach walked up to the ticket counter. An old man sat behind the counter, sitting on a wooden stool, reading the afternoon newspaper. "Hello, you lazy hound."

Jim Matthews looked up from his newspaper, recognized Momma Peach's loving face, and smiled. "Taking a trip, Momma Peach?" he teased.

Momma Peach leaned her right elbow onto the front counter and cast a strict eye at Jim. "If I was, you would be the last to know, Jim Matthews. I'm still upset with you because you ate Mrs. Bellman's blueberry cobbler instead of my peach pie at the church picnic."

Jim leaned forward and whispered: "And you know what, Momma Peach?"

"What?"

"Mrs. Bellman's blueberry cobbler was just awful, too," he said and then chuckled to himself. "But the things we men do when courting a widow."

Momma Peach grinned. "Oh, yes," she agreed. "Now, tell me, has any soul been in to see you today?"

"Nathan Hardy is leaving town today. You know that boy got a scholarship to go to college down there in Florida? He better hurry his butt up, too. The driver arrives early and leaves right on the second."

"Nathan Hardy?" Momma Peach asked and searched her memory. "Oh, Hank and Kathy Hardy's boy."

"Good people," Jim said with a nod. He rubbed his right elbow, stood up, straightened out the white and gray work shirt he was wearing and looked at Michelle. "Who are you looking for, Detective?"

Before Michelle could speak, Betty stepped through the front door of the building wearing a fashionable blue dress. Instead of appearing frightened, she marched right up to the ticket counter, set down a gray suitcase next to where Momma Peach stood, and looked at Jim: "One ticket to Jacksonville, please."

Momma Peach examined Betty carefully. She sniffed the air and caught the scent of a cheap perfume floating off of Betty. "You've been down to Flora's Hair Place, haven't you? Only Flora uses that perfumed shampoo I smell coming from you."

Betty didn't look at Momma Peach. "My business is my business," she said in a sharp tone.

"Hello again, Betty. When I saw you earlier your gray hair hadn't seen the inside of a hair salon in probably a couple years," Michelle told Betty. "Now your hair looks considerably nicer. Also, if I recall, your hair was gray. Now it's brown."

"So what?" Betty asked Michelle. "Is it against the law to get your hair done in this town?"

"No," Michelle said. "But I wish you'd told me you were leaving town. Don't you know that looks suspicious in an investigation? By the way, I like your dress. I saw one just like it in the front display window at Clair's Boutique."

"Mighty pricey, that place," Momma Peach commented.

"You gonna sell me a ticket or what?" Betty snapped at Jim.

"No, he isn't," Michelle told Betty and pointed at the wooden bench. "Sit down."

"Are you arresting me?"

"I want to talk," Michelle said.

"Arrest me or get lost," Betty told Michelle in a hateful tone.

"Oh, no you didn't," Momma Peach said. Before Betty knew what was happening, Momma Peach had swung her pocketbook over her shoulder and landed a blow squarely between Betty's shoulder blades. "Get over there and sit down!" Momma Peach yelled in a furious voice. "Nobody, and I mean nobody, talks to my baby like that!"

Betty scurried toward the bench and threw her hands in the air to block Momma Peach's attack. "Are you crazy?!" she yelled.

"I'm about to get more than crazy if the situation calls for me to be!" Momma Peach yelled back. Michelle grinned at Jim. Jim smiled, sat back down on his stool, and returned his attention to his newspaper.

Betty backed up to the wooden bench and tumbled down right as Momma Peach's pocketbook went flying past her head. "You're insane!"

Michelle approached, put a gentle hand on Momma

Peach's shoulder, and looked down at Betty. "Who paid you to leave town?" she asked.

"I don't know what you're talking about," Betty hissed and began rubbing her shoulder. "You should arrest this woman for assault."

"I don't think so. Her methods might be unorthodox, but it looks to me like Momma Peach just prevented a suspect in a murder case from escaping," Michelle informed Betty in a pointed tone. "I told you this morning to stay in town."

"You also said I wasn't under arrest," Betty said defensively and looked up at Momma Peach. "You had no right to attack me."

"Be grateful I didn't have a frying pan handy," Momma Peach told Betty and put her pocketbook down at her feet. "A poor soul is dead. Haven't you got a conscience, woman?"

"I didn't know the man," Betty replied in a sour voice. "I found him dead...over one of your pies if I recall. Maybe you killed him, huh?"

Momma Peach bent down, put her nose to Betty's nose and said: "Don't ever insult one of my famous peach pies again, woman. You will wish you didn't live long enough to regret it."

Betty's eyes grew wide and the whites of her eyes were stark around her pupils. "I just meant—"

"I know what you meant," Momma Peach said and stood back up. "Listen here, Miss High and Mighty. You have a piece of steak stuck in your teeth and your breath smells like an Andes mint like they give out down at the chop house. New dress, fancy haircut, steak lunch, and now you're buying a ticket to Jacksonville. Cleaning rooms at a slum motel must pay nicely."

"I'm sure a lie detector test will tell us what we need to know," Michelle told Momma Peach.

"What? Wait, no..." Betty said in a nervous voice. Tiny beads of sweat broke out on her forehead, plainly visible in the harsh overhead light of the bus depot. "I haven't done anything wrong, honest. I didn't kill that man...I..."

"You what?" Momma Peach demanded.

Betty cast her eyes down at her hands. "You don't understand... I've lived a hard life. I was married to an abusive husband for twenty years. Sure, I drank a lot with him and caused a lot of grief for myself by not divorcing the jerk when he first started hitting me...but I didn't have no place to go." Betty shook her head. "I was raised white trash...I only went as far as the eighth grade... I can barely read and write...so what if my husband hit me? At least he kept me around."

Momma Peach saw tears begin falling from Betty's eyes.

Her heart broke for the woman. "I understand," she said and sat down next to Betty and put her right arm around her. Betty flinched. "I'm not going to hurt you. You just keep talking."

Betty looked into Momma Peach's eyes. "I didn't mean what I said about your pie," she promised. "I was being mean."

"I know."

Betty ducked her head down, ashamed of herself. "I've been on my own for the last five years. Garth, that was my husband, got liquored up one night and ran his truck through a red light." Betty explained and wiped at her tears. "When he went to jail, I got kicked out of our apartment. I didn't have no money. So I called my cousin...he's the guy who owns the motel. He let me stay there in exchange for cleaning the rooms."

"Why didn't you tell me he was your cousin?" Michelle demanded.

"Because I got to look out for myself," Betty snapped at Michelle.

"Now, let's be calm," Momma Peach pleaded.

"Calm?" Betty laughed. "How can I be calm when I'm scared half to death?"

"Why?" Michelle asked.

"Because I was told to leave town or die," Betty answered Michelle in a hard voice. "But, as you can see, I was treated very nicely when I decided to leave town. I was given a lot of money. I sure don't know why but I didn't ask any questions."

"That was blackmail," Michelle explained. "You took the bribe and now if you decide to talk then they've got leverage against you."

"That's right," Momma Peach said. "You also mark yourself as a guilty, guilty person."

"If you left town I would suspect you killed Mr. Graystone and put a warrant out for your arrest, too," Michelle added. "Of course, the person who paid you off knows this."

"You mean... I was being set up?" Betty asked, comprehension dawning on her face.

Momma Peach nodded. "Seems that way," she said.

"But what choice did I have?" Betty begged. "My life was threatened."

"Of course it was," Momma Peach told Betty and gently pulled her closer. "I know how a snake thinks. You think of yourself as a piece of white trash, uneducated, and unworthy of love. So along comes a snake who spots your weakness and attacks without mercy. But don't worry, I know how to kill that kind of snake." Momma Peach looked up into Michelle's thoughtful face. "We need to make folks around here think Betty has left town."

"I was thinking the same thing," Michelle agreed. She placed a gentle hand on Betty's shoulder. "Floyd Garland paid you off, didn't he?"

"I'll die if I tell you," Betty answered in a scared voice. "Money talks and even I know that you cops can't protect me from the power of money."

"God is more powerful than all the money in the world," Momma Peach promised Betty. "You just nod your head yes or no when I ask you this question: Did Floyd Garland pay you to leave town?"

Betty looked deep into Momma Peach's eyes. Something in the woman's eyes brought courage and comfort to her terrified heart. She quickly nodded her head. "That's why that snake didn't show up at the police station with Felicia," Michelle said in an angry voice. "And more than likely he's parked outside somewhere watching the bus station. I could arrest him, but we need hard evidence about the murder. All we have is evidence of blackmail."

"His lawyer would have him walking in less than an hour," Momma Peach said in a calm tone. She patted Betty's hand. "Go buy your ticket, and get on the bus. But get off in Dawnville. I will be there to pick you up."

"And bring me back here?" Betty asked. "No deal. Please, just let me leave town. I'm going to Jacksonville. That's where I was raised. I have enough money to rent an apartment. I can get a job cleaning hotels. Please...just let me go," Betty begged.

"And go back to drinking at bars, being used by abusive men, and ending up dead in an alley? I don't think so," Momma Peach told Betty sternly.

"Why do you care?" Betty asked. "I'm a nobody...a booze hound...a washed-up piece of trash on the beach that people kick to the side. What does it matter where I end up?" She looked down at her fine blue dress and for a moment she crumpled a handful of the material in one fist as if she wanted to rip it off and expose her true self beneath.

"It matters to me," Momma Peach told Betty and placed her right hand to Betty's cheek. "I care."

Without understanding why, Betty burst into tears and threw her arms around Momma Peach. Momma Peach pulled Betty into her loving arms and held her. "You're going to come live with me," she whispered in Betty's ear. "I'll keep you safe and set you right. But first I need you to get on that bus and make Floyd Garland think you left town. I will pick you up in Dawnville."

"Please," Michelle begged Betty. She squatted down close to Betty. "You're not alone anymore if you don't want to be."

Betty nodded. "Okay...I'll do it."

Outside, parked at a safe distance down the street in his flashy red BMW, Floyd Garland waited for Betty to leave the bus station and get on the Greyhound bus. When Betty walked outside with Michelle and Momma Peach at her side, he tensed up. But then he saw Michelle speak to the driver, who stepped out to place Betty's suitcase under the bus in the luggage compartment, then she shook Betty's hand and walked back inside the bus station with Momma Peach. Betty boarded the bus just as she'd promised him. He kept watch, wary that she might change her mind at the last second, but all he saw was that five minutes later a young man came running up and managed to catch the bus before it pulled away. "We'll talk tomorrow," Floyd whispered at Michelle as he drove away from the bus station and tailed the Greyhound bus until it reached the interstate. "Don't come back," he warned Betty, before pulling an illegal U-turn and speeding back toward town.

Momma Peach relaxed as Michelle drove down a scenic country road that wound past fields and farms. The back roads were pretty, quiet, and controlled by a safe speed limit. The interstate, oh heavens give her strength, was filled with race car drivers escaping one deadly accident after another only because they stayed in between two painted lines. "This is as pretty as a picture. I don't like the interstate," she told Michelle, looking out at a wide view of picturesque green fields dotted with bales of hay. "And those big trucks scare me."

"Teenagers scare me worse," Michelle replied with a snort of laughter.

Momma Peach chuckled to herself. "You got that right. Should be a law against giving a sixteen-year-old child a license to drive. Most teenagers today can't even get out of bed without being slapped across the head a few good times. No way am I going to get on a busy interstate with big trucks and pimple-faced teenagers. And don't get me started on the old folk...oh, give me strength."

Momma Peach rolled down her window and took in a deep breath of the fresh bales of hay sitting in the beautiful green field. The hay smelled like summer. Momma Peach delighted in the smell. She looked up in adoration at the way the sun in the blue sky above seemed to shine down and tickle the hay with loving fingers. "Sometimes I forget to do that," Michelle commented to Momma Peach, watching her for a moment.

"You mean, to enjoy God's creation?" Momma Peach asked.

"Yes. Sometimes...I get so used to seeing the ugly side of life that I forget that there's still art out there to admire."

"God is the greatest artist of all," Momma Peach smiled and patted Michelle's knee. "See those bales of hay?"

Michelle slowed down the Oldsmobile and looked into the field. "Yes."

"God's hay," Momma Peach smiled from ear to ear. "The grass, the sky, the trees, the birds, the hay, you and me, all God's. Nothing on this earth is man's. No sir," Momma Peach said. "The houses we live in come from material already put on this earth by God Himself. Man might think he's smart because he can put a picture on a television screen, but where did that television screen come from, huh? I see God in all things because God created all things through Jesus."

"You should have been a preacher."

"The Lord has other uses for me," Momma Peach told Michelle and patted her knee again. "Sometimes, if we forget to look at God's beauty we can become like Betty, that poor soul. I sure have my work cut out for me."

"Are you sure you want that woman staying with you, Momma Peach?" Michelle asked worriedly.

Momma Peach nodded. "Unless I help that poor soul she'll end up drinking herself to death in the bars."

"Seems like that's all she wants anyway."

"No," Momma Peach said and looked out at a two-story farm house. She spotted two kids standing in the driveway throwing a football while a lazy old dog watched. Behind the farmhouse stood a large red barn filled with more bales of hay. "That poor soul needs someone to show her love. If we desert her she'll desert herself. I know you understand that."

"I do, Momma Peach," Michelle said in a wistful voice, thinking of how Momma Peach had been there for her through her own struggles. "But honestly, is it our fault Betty is the way she is? She could have left her husband, gone to night school, got her GED, attended college. I know people who came from worse than she ever had that ended up with a master's degree. I believe in showing people compassion...and I don't mind showing Betty compassion...but it really ticks me off to see people like her hiding behind a wall of dumb excuses."

"Some folk just never believe they'll ever be good enough," Momma Peach told Michelle. "Some folk just think all they'll ever be is trash. And this old world doesn't help to change their opinion. Betty is a broken woman, mostly because she believes the worst about herself instead of daring to find the good that is hiding in her heart."

Michelle looked at Momma Peach. "What are your plans, Momma Peach? Are you going to push Betty to go back to school? Allow her to work in your bakery? What?"

"None of the above," Momma Peach replied. "I'm going to let her breathe and figure out her own path."

"Just be careful she doesn't play you like a fiddle. Betty's kind can be slippery."

"I know that," Momma Peach said in a careful voice that told Michelle that she had seen more characters in her life, bad and good, than she would ever know.

Michelle was silent for a few minutes, thinking. "I'm really trusting you, Momma Peach. If Betty isn't at the bus station in Dawnville I'm in a world of trouble."

"She'll be there."

"I pray you're right," Michelle told Momma Peach. "I spotted a man sitting in a red BMW sitting across the street from the bus station."

"Floyd Garland." Momma Peach looked like she had accidentally bit into a sour pickle when she was expecting a sweet one.

"Yes," Michelle said.

Momma Peach bit down on her lip. "I don't like bullies."

"Neither do I," Michelle stated. "Momma Peach?"

"Yes?"

"Mr. Graystone was killed for his money," Michelle said. "That I'm sure of. But why was he here in our town? What was he doing? The killer obviously knew he was in town, too."

"Maybe not until the very end," Momma Peach pointed out.

"What do you mean?"

Momma Peach reached down into her pocketbook and pulled out a mint. "Mr. Graystone was married to a wealthy woman. This woman, according to Felicia Garland, was half blind and shouldn't have been allowed to drive." Momma Peach placed the mint into her mouth. "Mr. Graystone, rest his soul, let his wife drive. Now, whether he allowed her to do that on purpose or not, I don't know. But what I do know is that Mr. Graystone was worth a lot of the green stuff that poisons this world and his daughter was very bitter at him."

"But...?" Michelle said, reading the hesitation in Momma Peach's voice.

"I don't believe Felicia Garland wanted her father dead, but I do believe she knows why her father was in town."

"All arrows point at Floyd Garland."

"Yes, they do," Momma Peach agreed. "We're going to dig around Floyd Garland until we find what he doesn't want us to find. We need to see what skeletons we find in his closets."

"This is a very messy case," Michelle said, shaking her head. "Floyd Garland is a wealthy man. Unless we have concrete evidence to convict him with, Momma Peach, the army of lawyers he'll hire on his behalf will chew us up and spit us out."

"I know," Momma Peach replied in a calm voice. "That's why I am going to let Betty draw the snake into the house." Momma Peach grew quiet and focused on her thoughts. "Michelle?"

"Yes?"

"What if," Momma Peach asked in a low, thoughtful voice, "Mr. Graystone and Felicia Garland were both out to kill Floyd Garland? Now, before you answer, what I said is just a thought that I can't back up with any evidence."

Michelle looked over at Momma Peach. "What if?"

"But what if Floyd Garland interrupted that plan and killed Mr. Graystone, rest his soul, because he wanted the poor man's money? We have some dangerous paths to explore, don't we?"

"We sure do," Michelle agreed as they drove into the city limits of Dawnville. She passed a Krispy Creme, a few fast food restaurants, and a grocery store, then stopped at a red light. Dawnville was a small town. "Not much in this town," Michelle told Momma Peach, craning her neck to look around from the intersection.

"Some good folk live here," Momma Peach said and looked at a long white brick building sitting off to the side of a chain diner. "I used to come here as a small child, when the only thing here was a gas station and that old building over there."

Michelle followed the direction of Momma Peach's gaze. "Why did you come here?"

"Used to be a drive-in right there," Momma Peach smiled as her eyes filled with warm memories. "Oh, I would come here and watch the worst horror movies ever made by man, but it was fun. I'd sit under the stars, drink soda, eat popcorn, laugh and talk with old friends...those were the days. Simpler times."

The red light turned green. Michelle eased the Oldsmobile forward through the intersection and started to look around for the bus station. "I'm surprised this town has a bus station."

"Lot of kids leave these small towns as soon as they turn eighteen," Momma Peach said in a sad voice. "Small towns like this might not look like much, but they give the bus lines good business. Some of them go off to college, or the Army. I worry about the kids who follow their dreams to California and think they'll become movie stars but end up broken instead. Bus line doesn't care about that part, though."

"Business is business," Michelle said. "You can't blame a taxi cab driver for taking a drunk to a bar."

"No, you can't," Momma Peach sighed and pointed to her

right. "There," she said. Michelle spotted a small white wooden building with a Greyhound sign outside. She hit her blinker and turned into the parking lot.

"We're about twenty minutes behind the bus. Betty should be here." Michelle's brow furrowed with worry.

Momma Peach nodded. "Yes, she should," she said and searched the parking lot carefully for Betty. All she saw was a run-down red truck parked to one side of the building. Michelle parked beside the red truck. "Let's look inside. Maybe the bus is late?"

Michelle nodded her head. She got out of the Oldsmobile and walked into the humble lobby that smelled of cheap disinfectant and moldy carpeting. Three men who reeked of cigarette smoke stood near a line of five metal chairs talking together; each man was wearing a leather bikers jacket with a black widow stitched on the back. The men looked over at Momma Peach and then at Michelle. "Hey, good looking," one man with a rough, scarred face and yellowed teeth catcalled, "why don't you come over here and sit on Papa's lap."

Momma Peach prepared her pocketbook for the attack. She charged up to the man with fire and brimstone in her eyes and Michelle knew the men had no idea what was coming. "I don't like the way you're talking," she said and walloped the man across his face. "Have some respect."

The man stepped back and laughed as if it were nothing.

"Cool it, momma," he said and nodded his head at his two friends, "we're not interested in you. We want that pretty chick over there."

"It's okay, Momma Peach," Michelle said in a cool voice that told Momma Peach to stand back. And that's exactly what she did as Michelle walked up to the three men. "You jerks want a fight?"

"Check her out," the man snickered to his friends, "the little chick wants to fight the big bad wolf." The two other men laughed back and slowly began circling Michelle like hungry buzzards. Michelle took off her tailored leather jacket and tossed it to Momma Peach. Her badge was in her back pocket and she didn't wear a gun holster, so they still had no idea what they were in for. "Oh, what are you gonna do?" the man mocked Michelle as he stopped smiling. "Are you gonna teach Papa Bear a big bad lesson?" The man nodded his head at his two friends. "Teach her a lesson. I'll take the leftovers."

The two men grinned and moved toward Michelle. Michelle dropped down into a defensive position, swung her leg around, and kicked one of the men square in the face. The man went flying backward. The second man charged at Michelle. Michelle spun and slid into a perfect split as she flung both of her fists out at the same time, punching the man in the gut and knocking the breath out of him. Before the man could recover, Michelle flung herself up in a back flip, landed on her feet, brought her right leg around in a perfect roundhouse kick. Her attacker went flying sideways and landed heavily on the floor.

"Oh, you're gonna pay, big time," the man with the yellowed teeth promised Michelle. He reached into the right pocket of his jacket and pulled out a switchblade. "Time to bleed."

Momma Peach spotted the first man beginning to get up. She ran over to him and began beating him with her pocketbook. "Stay down, you dirty dog," she growled at him. The man threw his hands up over his head and hunkered down, not daring to get up.

"So what are you waiting for?" Michelle asked her attacker with a cold smile.

The man hissed and stabbed the switchblade toward Michelle with lightning-fast hands. But Michelle was quicker. As he moved forward, she brought her right foot up, kicked the man's hand so that he almost dropped the knife, and followed through with a roundhouse punch to the nose. Meanwhile Momma Peach kept one eye on her baby girl's progress while she continued to beat the first man down, adding in blows for the second man who began trying to get up as well. "Stay down!" she hissed.

The man with the knife felt his nose and grimaced in pain and fury. "Die," he snarled at Michelle and then charged toward her. Michelle narrowed her eyes and waited for the perfect moment. All Momma Peach saw was Michelle's attacker's knife go flying as she landed a flurry of punches on his face followed by three vicious roundhouse kicks and one last front kick to the chest. "That's it, baby!" she yelled and watched as Michelle's attacker landed flat on his face. His two friends, seeing this, finally scrambled away from Momma Peach's blows and ran out of the lobby. Michelle walked over to the man lying unconscious on the floor and slapped handcuffs on him. "Time to go to prison for assaulting and intending to murder a cop with a deadly weapon," Michelle said, barely breathing heavily as she waited for him to wake up so she could read him his rights.

Momma Peach walked over to Michelle, smiling from ear to ear, and patted her on the shoulder. "That's my baby," she said proudly.

A skittish woman in her late fifties eased out of a side door beside the ticket counter. "I...I called the cops," she said. "You better leave."

"I'm a cop," Michelle said to the woman and presented her badge.

The woman approached Michelle and examined her badge. "Oh, you must be that detective from the next town that everyone talks about...the martial arts expert."

"I guess," Michelle said and put her badge away, suppressing a smile. She didn't like to brag but it was nice to have a little notoriety for the amount of training she had put in toward her martial arts and fighting skills. "More importantly, has the bus arrived yet?"

Momma Peach prepared for the worst. She just knew her big old heart was going to cause Michelle trouble. "We want the truth," she told the woman.

"Not yet," the woman said. "There was an accident on the interstate."

Michelle glanced at Momma Peach. Momma Peach sighed in relief and smiled. "Thank you," she said to the woman. "By the way, let your hair down out of that ugly bun you have it in. You'll look so much prettier that way."

The woman looked surprised, but she smiled and lifted her right hand to touch her long black hair that was wrapped into a tight bun. "Thanks," she told Momma Peach. "I guess I always thought, why bother if Prince Charming doesn't exactly hang out at the bus station? But you're right. I've always loved my hair down." She walked back to the ticket counter, letting her hair down as she went.

Michelle looked down at the unconscious man lying at her feet. "Momma Peach?" she asked.

"Yes?"

"Thanks for your help," Michelle said and looked at

Momma Peach with worry in her eyes. "Those two men could have hurt you."

"Michelle," Momma Peach said and wrapped her arm lovingly around Michelle's shoulders, "you know not one grown man has ever stood up to my pocketbook when I have the wrath on me. They got what was coming to them. All that matters is that I was there to stand by my baby."

Michelle leaned her head on Momma Peach's shoulder and closed her eyes. Five minutes later, two cops ran into the lobby with their guns drawn, a lot of tedious explanations to make.

After twenty minutes, the bus pulled into the parking lot. And then Momma Peach walked back to Michelle's Oldsmobile empty-handed. Betty, she was told by the bus driver, had insisted she be let off on the detour exit the bus was forced to take. "Me and my silly old heart," Momma Peach said, walking to the Oldsmobile. "Now what am I going to do?"

CHAPTER FOUR

*M*omma Peach wearily set her pocketbook down on the counter in the kitchen at the back of her bakery. Mandy walked up behind Momma Peach and began massaging her shoulders. "You look like you're tired to the bone."

"Oh, I feel like I've been run through the ringer," Momma Peach said and leaned her neck back. "A little to the left...yes, that's the spot."

"The store is swept up, the cash drawer is counted down, and the bank deposit is in the safe," Mandy told Momma Peach. "The bakery did really good today. We sold out of your peach bread and peach pie."

"Oh, I will bake more up tonight," Momma Peach promised. "Do you have any plans for tonight?"

"I have to study some, and then soak in a hot bath, and

afterward listen to my mother lecture me about being single," Mandy sighed. "It's not like I want to be single, Momma Peach. Boys at the community college, well, they're interested in pretty girls who go around in those jogging shorts that don't cover half their butts."

Momma Peach turned around and put her hands on Mandy's slender shoulders. "Those types of boys you don't need anyway," she told Mandy in a stern tone. "God will send you the right man when the time is right, so don't go chasing after boys."

"I just get lonely sometimes," Mandy confessed. "My mother seems to think I'm considering a career as a nun, even though I'm Baptist. I don't understand why she can't accept that being single at twenty is not that big of a deal. I mean, I dated in high school...some. I went to the prom, even though it was with the nerdiest kid in school. I..." Mandy stopped and dropped her head down onto Momma Peach's soft shoulder. "I'm a nerd," she moaned miserably.

Momma Peach smiled fondly. "You are not a nerd. You are a very, very special child of God." Momma Peach patted Mandy's head with her hand. "Oh, my sweet children, what am I going to do with you all."

The sound of someone knocking on the front door of the bakery caused Mandy to raise her head. "Who could that be?"

"Let me find out. You leave through the back door," Momma Peach ordered Mandy.

Mandy hesitated. "Momma Peach, maybe I should hang around a little bit longer?"

"Go home," Momma Peach told Mandy and kissed her cheek. "I will call you later to say goodnight."

Mandy glanced at the back door and then nodded. She knew better than to stand around and argue with Momma Peach. "Bye," she said and hugged Momma Peach. "Goodnight."

Momma Peach waited a moment until Mandy left and then walked into the front of the bakery. Floyd Garland was standing outside in an expensive, gray overcoat and a dark gray fedora hat. "So, the dog comes prowling," Momma Peach whispered. She walked over to the front door of the bakery and disengaged the lock. "Give me strength," she prayed and opened the front door a crack. "We're closed."

Floyd Garland regarded Momma Peach with cold eyes and then put on a businesslike smile that was so fake it could have caused a two-year-old to vomit up his lunch. "Momma Peach, right?" he asked.

Momma Peach stared into the eyes of a poisonous snake. "Yes," she said and decided to use honey instead of vinegar. She swallowed down her disgust and smiled. "And who are you?"

"I'm Floyd Garland. I'm the mortgage clerk down at the bank," Floyd told Momma Peach in a voice that attempted to sound sweet and pleasant but came out overcooked and rotted instead. "May I come in?"

Momma Peach glanced up and down the front sidewalk. No one was in sight and the sun was beginning to set behind the tall pine trees lining the street. "We can talk right here," she said and closed the front door behind her. "It's so stuffy in my bakery. The air is fresh out here and there's a nice breeze this evening."

Floyd nodded his head. "I agree," he said and pointed to a cast iron table and chairs sitting off to the right side of the porch in front of the display window. "May we sit down?"

"If you like," Momma Peach said. She walked over to the table and sat down with her back against the building of the bakery. The row of cozy stores across the street were closing down. The birds were settling down for a gentle night of sleep. The sky was yawning with twilight overhead and the trees were pulling shadows across their limbs. Momma Peach wanted nothing more than to fetch a cup of warm tea, sit outside her bakery, and watch her town fall asleep. Instead, she was sitting across from a man with a polluted soul. "What is it that you want to talk about?"

Floyd sat down across from Momma Peach and clasped his hands together. "I want to talk business," he said in a voice that was serious and calculated. "I want to talk about your bakery."

"My bakery?" Momma Peach asked and her eyes widened in surprise.

"Yes," Floyd said. "You own the building your bakery is housed in, correct?"

"Yes. I bought this building with a business loan that I paid off ten years ago."

Floyd nodded his head. "It has been brought to my attention that there was an error with the processing of the business loan."

Momma Peach braced herself to be bombarded with his threatening lies. "Oh? An error?"

"It seems," Floyd continued smoothly, "that the mortgage clerk at the time miscalculated your interest rate. You were given a much lower interest rate than allowed." Floyd leaned across the table and lowered his voice. "Regrettably, the difference must be paid. Over the length of the original loan, plus the ten years since then, using the correct interest rate, you have accumulated a great amount of debt."

"I see," Momma Peach replied, remaining calm in the face of his sinister attack. "How much debt, exactly?"

"As it stands, and will stand in a court of law," Floyd said in a threatening tone tainted with glee, "you owe the bank over twenty-five thousand dollars that is due within two weeks or the bank will be forced to repossess your bakery and sell it."

"I see," Momma Peach said, resisting the urge to reach across the table and pull Floyd's ears off his head. "Maybe there are other options for me?" she asked innocently.

"There are always options," Floyd said and leaned back, satisfied. "For instance, option one could be to focus on baking bread and nothing else. Perhaps the judge might take some pity on you when we bring it to court."

"What would be my other options? I ain't that smart, you see. You would know better than me." She turned her wide brown eyes on him in supplication and waited for the snake to enter the trap. She reflected that perhaps she wouldn't need Betty to entrap this prey, or perhaps not yet.

Floyd nodded as he settled comfortably in his chair. Momma Peach knew he moved in such rich circles that he probably wasn't even aware of her reputation as a brilliant detective. He saw her as a fly to be swatted out of the way and nothing more. "A friend of mine left town today. I just happened to see you at the bus station with her," he told Momma Peach in a slithery voice. "I was unaware that my friend knew you. That's where option two comes in. Perhaps if you forget about my friend and bake your little pies, then maybe I can arrange to fix this error in the paperwork. Of course, if you keep sticking your nose into business where it don't belong, then, unfortunately, that back payment money may come back to haunt you, and it may rise significantly." He made a little face as if the whole matter was distasteful to him, and waited for her to take the bait.

Momma Peach listened to a pretty bird sing into the approaching night from a pine tree in front of her bakery. She knew to make Mr. Garland wait. She spotted Mrs. Hensley across the street locking up her bookstore. "Hey there, Mrs. Hensley," she called out and waved. Mrs. Hensley waved back, walked across the street, and greeted Momma Peach.

"I came over about an hour ago to buy some peach bread but Mandy told me you were all out," Mrs. Hensley said and looked over at Floyd. "Oh, am I interrupting something?"

"Nothing important," Momma Peach promised with a serene smile. "I'll have some fresh bread out tomorrow bright and early, Mrs. Hensley. My, for a woman of seventy you're looking mighty tempting in that yellow dress. You should be ashamed of yourself. Every man in this town will be knocking on your door tonight to take a peek at that dress."

Mrs. Hensley blushed. "Momma Peach, the only man knocking on my door tonight will be my husband coming in from work asking about his dinner."

"I know, I know," Momma Peach chuckled. "How is Harry?"

"Cranky and old," Mrs. Hensley said with a stern look that was nevertheless humorous. "I swear that man thinks my kitchen is nothing more than a place to fuss about his aches and pains. I've asked him to retire more times than I can remember now, but he refuses."

"I'm sure Harry just doesn't want to give up making furniture," Momma Peach assured Mrs. Hensley. "Oh, by the way, this is Mr. Floyd from the bank. We're talking about my bakery. Would you believe this – it seems that I owe some money to the bank because Mr. Hillson, the man who helped me make my business loans years back, made a mistake and gave me an interest rate that the bank didn't approve of? Seems I owe twenty-five thousand dollars in back payments."

Floyd tensed up in his seat. Before he could say a word, Mrs. Hensley tore into him. "That's outrageous. Why I'll go down and talk to Mr. Finney at the bank myself first thing tomorrow morning and tell him where he can shove his money if he wants to pull that kind of dirty trick on a good honest business woman like you, Momma Peach. I'll close down my business account and my personal account and take my business elsewhere. How dare you come here and insist she pay for your mistake." Mrs. Hensley turned to Momma Peach. "Don't worry, Momma Peach, we'll get you the best lawyer money can buy. We'll organize a business protest and boycott the bank and—"

"Mrs. Hensley," Floyd interrupted in a sharp voice, leaping to his feet, "that won't be necessary. It seems that there has been a mistake on my part. This was a terrible misunderstanding. Momma Peach doesn't owe the bank anything." Floyd looked down at Momma Peach and narrowed his eyes with unexpressed rage. "I'm sorry to have bothered you this fine evening."

"Oh, think nothing of it," Momma Peach grinned. "Tell Mr. Finney to say hello to Martha for me."

"Of course," Floyd said and walked away stiffly.

Mrs. Hensley huffed. "What was that all about?" she asked.

"Mrs. Hensley," Momma Peach stood up, "you are an amazing woman and a dear friend, do you know that? And I love you to pieces."

Mrs. Hensley watched Floyd disappear down the sidewalk. "That man doesn't sit right in my eyes, Momma Peach."

Momma Peach walked Mrs. Hensley back across the street and helped her into her gray Honda Accord. "You don't worry about that man," she told Mrs. Hensley. "Now, scooter-poot on home and get Harry his supper started. I'll have Mandy run you over a fresh loaf of my peach bread tomorrow."

Mrs. Hensley smiled up at Momma Peach. "You haven't been over for supper in a while. How about tomorrow night?"

Momma Peach patted Mrs. Hensley's hand with care. "In time," she promised. "Right now, I have business to tend to."

Momma Peach waved goodbye to Mrs. Hensley and walked back to her bakery. For the next three hours, she worked in her kitchen baking bread and pies. The scent of rising dough, cinnamon, brown sugar and peaches filled the air. Finally, when the last batch was out of the oven and she felt exhaustion overtake her, she walked home through a warm night buzzing with the lazy flicker of lightning bugs searching for love under a sky twinkling with bright summer stars. "I have a lot of work to do," Momma Peach told herself as she walked home and then yawned, "but right now I need some sleep." And sleep she did. She snored so loud the roof covering her home nearly lifted off into space.

The following morning Momma Peach walked back to her bakery through the cool morning air feeling refreshed and clear-minded. She found Mandy already waiting at the front door. "My, will you look at that dress," Momma Peach beamed.

Mandy smiled. "I know green isn't really my color, but I like it."

"Green is you," Momma Peach promised Mandy and hugged her neck. "Now, tell me, what are you doing standing at the front door to my bakery so early the birds are still yawning?"

Mandy looked down at her hands. "I had a fight with my mom last night," she admitted. "And of course my dad didn't help much."

"Tell me."

"Oh," Mandy said and stomped at the sidewalk, "my mom invited that intolerable Matt Richardson over to our house last night. She thinks Matt is the answer to my being single, forgetting that I can't stand the guy. And I told him that, too...which didn't make my mom happy at all. When I woke up this morning she was still upset with me so I decided to come to work early."

Momma Peach sighed. "Oh," she said and pulled Mandy into her warm arms. "I wish I could make you feel better."

"Me, too."

Momma Peach looked over her shoulder and saw Michelle walk up carrying two brown paper cups of coffee and still wearing the same clothes from the day before. "Mandy, go inside." Momma Peach opened her pocketbook, took out the keys to the front door, and handed them to Mandy. "I baked some fresh bread and pies last night. Put them out, okay? And wrap one up extra special for Mrs. Hensley."

"Yes, Momma Peach," Mandy said. She took the keys from Momma Peach, unlocked the front door, and went inside.

"What is it?" Momma Peach asked Michelle with concern. "Your eyes are full of troubles. Tell me."

Michelle handed Momma Peach a cup of coffee and then looked up into the clear morning sky. "Betty Walker's body was found at a hotel in Fieldsdale," Michelle said in a heavy voice. "She was strangled to death, Momma Peach."

Momma Peach felt her heart break. Tears began streaming down from her tormented eyes. "Fieldsdale is the detour town that the bus stopped at yesterday, isn't it?"

Michelle nodded. "Yes."

"Oh, the poor baby," Momma Peach said. She wiped at her tears. "God rest her troubled soul. You went to Fieldsdale already?"

"Yes, Momma Peach," Michelle said and took a breath to

steady her exhausted mind. "The same cologne we smelled in the room Mr. Graystone was found in, Momma Peach, was in the room where Betty was killed."

"You smelled the cologne?" Momma Peach asked in alarm.

"Yes."

Momma Peach walked over to the table beside the display window and sat down. "I have news for you, too. Floyd Garland paid me a visit last night," she confessed. "Of course, thanks to my dear friend and angel Mrs. Hensley, his visit didn't turn out the way he planned." Despite her sadness about Betty's death, Momma Peach couldn't help but suppress a smirk to remember Floyd's poorly concealed rage as two women having a seemingly innocent neighborly chat had undone his sick little blackmail scheme.

Michelle sat down across from Momma Peach and worked on her coffee. She listened to Momma Peach describe the conversation she had had with Floyd Garland. "Seems like Mrs. Hensley really saved the day."

"Lovely woman, one of the best," Momma Peach said, thinking back again to Betty and how she'd never have a chance to improve her life. She fought back more tears as she remembered an important detail. "The cologne I smelled coming from Floyd Garland didn't match the money cologne I smelled in the room Mr. Graystone was killed in, rest his poor soul. The cologne I smelled on that snake Floyd Garland smelled expensive, but not as expensive as the cologne in the room Mr. Graystone was killed in."

Michelle leaned back in her chair. The morning was waking up as the sun rose higher and the air warmed up for another hot Georgia day. The birds were chirping far above them in the trees. At any other time, she would have cherished sitting in front of the bakery with Momma Peach, having coffee together. She could feel her fatigue pulling at her eyelids. "I'll speak with Floyd Garland today about noon. I want you to watch our conversation from the viewing room."

"I'll be there," Momma Peach promised. She sighed heavily. "Check the phone records at the hotel Betty was killed at. I have a bad feeling she called Floyd Garland."

"I already spoke to a Detective Mayfield. He's promised to share information with me," Michelle explained. "I'll give him a call after lunch and see what he's come up with."

"How did you find out about Betty Walker?" Momma Peach asked, forcing Michelle to focus. "Did this Detective Mayfield call you?"

"No, Momma Peach," Michelle said. She set down the coffee cup in her hand and looked at Momma Peach with mystified confusion in her eyes. "Are you ready for this?"

Momma Peach braced herself. "Hit me."

"I received an anonymous call," Michelle told Momma Peach. "Someone called me and told me that Betty Walker had been murdered. I was given the name of the hotel and the exact room number."

Momma Peach wiped away her tears and took this bit of information in solemnly. "We have more players in this game than we realized."

"I know."

"Time for me to tighten the strap on my thinking cap and start tossing some serious thinking into the oven," Momma Peach said and took a determined sip of her coffee. "I don't like being toyed with, no sir."

A beautiful brown finch looked down at Momma Peach from a tall tree limb, smiled, and flew away on the soft, morning breeze.

Momma Peach situated herself on a chair in the viewing room, reached into her pocketbook, pulled out a mint, and settled her mind. "I'm going to watch you carefully," she said, looking through the one-way mirror at Floyd Garland.

Floyd Garland had walked into the interrogation room without Felicia, sat down, and folded his hands across his chest. Michelle stepped in behind him, closed the door, and leaned against the back wall instead of sitting down. She examined Floyd with quick eyes that were in sharp contrast to her relaxed posture. The man was wearing a very expensive cream linen summer suit whose very tailoring seemed designed to intimidate. His short red hair was combed neatly and slicked back with a thin layer of gel that seemed to shimmer under the light just like his dark, snakelike eyes. Yet, Michelle noticed, the man was handsome – but not in an attractive way; Floyd's handsomeness was like a weapon that he wielded as part of his malice, so what might have been attractive was instead poisoned by hatred. "Thank you for coming down," she said finally.

"I would have accompanied my wife yesterday, but I had urgent business at the bank. I'm sure you understand, Detective," Floyd told Michelle in a smooth but cold tone that told her he wished to appear relaxed and friendly.

Momma Peach, watching through the mirrored window, knew better. "Liar," Momma Peach said and popped the mint in her hand into her mouth. "I'm going to get you good."

"Seems like your work has been keeping you very busy. I was informed you paid Momma Peach a visit late yesterday evening," Michelle said and folded her arms across her chest. "Mrs. Hensley was a witness to your visit, I understand. Strange, I thought bankers went home when the bank closed."

Floyd stiffened slightly in his chair. By now he had surely realized that his attempted threat against Momma Peach had created a weak ankle that he would have to keep walking on, somehow. "Yes, well," he said, "I thought it was urgent business that I inform Momma Peach of a banking matter involving her bakery. As it turned out, it was nothing to worry about. No harm, no foul."

Michelle nodded her head. She let the sleaze think his flimsy explanation had passed muster, but she had more important matters to cover and was going to enjoy watching him squirm. "Betty Walker informed me that you paid her to leave town. Is that true?"

"Who is Betty Walker?" Floyd asked in an innocent tone that rang false to her ears.

"The woman who found the dead body of Mr. Graystone. I'm sure you know who Mr. Graystone is, right?"

"Get him," Momma Peach whispered and bit down on the mint in her mouth so it snapped into two pieces.

"Yes, I'm aware of who that man is," Floyd said and shook his head. "Such a shame," he said. "I didn't know the man personally, mind you, but for him to be killed right here in our own little town...such a shame. And his death has not been easy on my wife, either, Detective. Felicia has been very upset and—"

"Betty Walker stated that you paid her to leave town and now she is dead," Michelle interrupted Floyd and his casual lies. She pushed up off the wall, planted her hands on the table across from him, and looked Floyd straight in his eyes. "I want some answers."

"Talk to my attorney," Floyd said to Michelle with a hint of steel gleaming behind the smoothness of his voice. "I am here of my own free will and I don't have to say a single word. Even if you arrest me I have the right to remain silent, Detective. And I will not be intimidated by this ridiculous charade. You don't have a shred of evidence. And whoever this...Betty Walker is...the woman is obviously a liar."

Michelle narrowed her eyes. "You're going to prison," she whispered in a voice so low that only Floyd heard her.

"Do not threaten me," Floyd warned Michelle. "I play rough."

"So do I," Michelle promised. She stood up straight and looked down at him. "I saw you at the bus station yesterday, Mr. Garland. You were there when Betty Walker boarded her bus. Later on, you visited Momma Peach and threatened to take her bakery away under the pretense of a very serious lie. That sounds like blackmail to me, with a nice touch of fraud. You also told Momma

Peach that you saw her at the bus station with a 'friend' you knew. What were you doing at the bus station, Mr. Garland?"

Floyd stiffened in his seat. "Again, talk to my attorney. Unless you intend to arrest me, I'll be leaving." But he did not rise from his seat.

"The only person Momma Peach was with at the bus station yesterday was Betty Walker," Michelle continued, ignoring his empty threats. "Strange how you paid Momma Peach a visit after bank hours to give her such terrible news and suddenly claimed it was a misunderstanding once Mrs. Hensley became witness to your visit. In fact, I plan to speak to Mr. Finney about your visit and ask him about bank protocol and see if your visit to Momma Peach was even authorized in the first place."

Floyd gritted his teeth. He was trapped. If Mr. Finney, the bank president, found out about his visit to Momma Peach, he would surely be terminated from his position at the bank. Also, Betty Walker was dead, and the Detective's line of thinking, while wrong, would easily sway a judge. He had little faith that even his well-paid lawyer could find him a way out of this mess. "I did not murder that woman. Talk to my attorney," he snarled.

"I guarantee you I will," Michelle said, her eyes never leaving Floyd's. "In the meantime, I'm placing you under arrest."

"On what grounds?" Floyd yelled and stormed to his feet. He balled his hands into fists and prepared to strike Michelle.

Michelle didn't waste a second. She lashed out with her right foot and aimed a kick at Floyd. As he ducked and the table slid forward, she jumped up onto it, swinging her right leg around to kick Floyd across his face. He went flying backward and crashed down against the back wall. Michelle crouched down on the table like a cat and looked at Floyd. "Never do that again," she warned him.

Floyd stared up at Michelle in shock. He had heard a rumor that the detective was a martial arts expert but had figured the rumors were widely exaggerated. But as he rubbed the side of his throbbing face and looked up into a pair of fierce eyes, he knew to pay attention from there on out. "I'll sue you for every sorry cent you're worth!" he yelled.

"You're under arrest for attempted assault against a police officer as well as suspicion of foul play. We'll talk about the blackmail and the fraud later. Betty Walker is dead. She claimed you paid her to leave town. You were at the bus station to ensure she left town. You threatened Momma Peach. And now Betty Walker is dead. Your attorney is going to have to dig really deep to even convince Judge Crump to let you make bail." Michelle jumped down from the table with her handcuffs in one hand. "I haven't even begun to connect you to the murder of Mr. Graystone."

"I didn't kill anyone," Floyd barked at Michelle as she cuffed his hands in front of him and helped him roughly to his feet. "I didn't even know the man was in town."

"Then why did you pay Betty Walker to leave town? Michelle asked. She sat him back down in his chair and returned to the other side of the table.

Floyd ran his cuffed hands through his slick red hair. "I—"

"Betty Walker found Mr. Graystone's body. She connects you to his murder," Michelle interrupted Floyd. "You better think smart, Mr. Garland, because everything you say is being recorded."

"I didn't kill anyone," Floyd insisted. His face turned pale as he looked up briefly, as if searching for the security cameras.

"Why did you pay Betty Walker to leave town?" Michelle repeated. She grabbed her chair and sat down. "Talk to me."

Floyd raised his cuffed hands to run the fingers of one hand through his hair again. He was in a world of trouble. "Okay," he said in a voice that was slowly losing power, "it's true...I paid Betty Walker to leave town. But I didn't bribe her to do it. She blackmailed me."

"Why?"

"Because she came to our home and threatened my wife, that's why," Floyd said in a voice that almost cracked with fatigue, desperation, and fury. "She said she would tell the police Felicia killed her old man if we didn't pay her a large sum of money."

"How did Betty Walker even know Mr. Graystone was related to your wife?" Michelle asked. This cast Betty in a whole new light and she glanced at the one-way mirror, wondering what Momma Peach was making of this new development. Was Floyd still just a snake and a manipulator, or was he finally revealing something useful?

"Who knows?" Floyd ranted. "I paid Momma Peach a visit because I couldn't have her sticking her nose where it didn't belong. If she convinced Betty to stay in town, I knew the whole thing would fall apart. I know what I did was wrong, but I had my wife to think about. Someone killed her old man," he said in a nervous voice, "and whoever that someone is could just as easily try and kill Felicia. So I paid Betty Walker the money and I made sure she left."

Momma Peach crossed her arms together and listened. "Don't reel him in yet," she whispered. "Let him talk."

"Betty Walker stated you threatened to kill her if she didn't leave town. We have two conflicting stories."

Michelle cocked her head to one side and regarded Floyd through narrowed eyes. She watched him sweat a little under the scrutiny.

"Who will a jury believe...a drunk motel cleaner or a respected member of the community?" Floyd asked Michelle and rubbed the side of his face again, trying to sit up straighter in his chair despite the evident pain. "Listen to me, Detective, I took drastic measures to ensure my wife remained safe. If that makes me a bad guy and gets me fired from the bank, then so be it."

Michelle watched Floyd attempt to paint himself as a worried husband instead of a criminal. She glanced over at the mirror and rolled her eyes for a split second. "Betty Walker is dead. Mr. Graystone is dead. You're my number one suspect."

"I didn't kill anyone."

"So you say," Michelle said. "I guess a lie detector test will tell me if you're being honest or not. Maybe you are...maybe you aren't."

Floyd stared at Michelle. Then he caved in, seeing it was his last, best option. "I...yes, okay, I'll take a lie test," he said. "I didn't kill Felicia's old man and I didn't kill Betty Walker. I may have acted...improperly...but my intentions were merely to protect my wife. Furthermore, I will apologize to Momma Peach personally and explain the true reason for my visit."

"He's a snake, be careful of him," Momma Peach whispered. "He's telling half-truths."

"There's a lot of questions we can answer right here before we get to the lie detector," Michelle told Floyd. "I want to know how Betty Walker knew Mr. Graystone was related to your wife...if," Michelle emphasized, "she did threaten you the way you claim. And if Betty Walker did threaten you, that must mean your wife knows more than she pretended to. I want to know where you went after you left Momma Peach's bakery."

"Home."

Michelle nodded. "I'll confirm the time with your wife. I also want to know where you were the night of the murder. But for now, I'm putting you on ice. Ted!"

A tall cop with a large pot belly stepped into the interrogation room. "Yeah, Detective?"

"Book Mr. Garland for attempted assault against a police officer. I'll handle the other charges I have against him later," Michelle explained. "He gets his one phone call to his attorney. We wouldn't want to forget that." She gave Floyd a cold smile that didn't reach her eyes. "Also, place him in a holding cell by himself. And no visitors."

"Yes, ma'am," the cop said and nodded his head at Floyd. "Let's go."

Floyd awkwardly stood up with his hands still cuffed in

front of him. "I'll have your badge," he snapped at Michelle as he was walked out of the room.

Michelle followed Floyd out of the interrogation room and was joined in her office moments later by Momma Peach. "Floyd Garland didn't kill Mr. Graystone. He didn't kill Betty Walker, either," Momma Peach said in a heavy voice. "But that don't make a snake innocent of eating a canary."

"I know," Michelle told Momma Peach and sat down on the edge of her desk. "He can get away with fooling around on a lie detector test, too. I just said that because I wanted to watch him squirm."

Momma Peach walked over to the window in the office and looked up at the clear blue sky of another perfect Georgia day. She stood still for a few minutes and listened to the birds fill the outside world with beautiful songs. "Michelle?"

"Yes?"

"I need to go to the bank," Momma Peach said. "I need to find the man wearing the money cologne."

Michelle looked at Momma Peach with a quizzical look. "What are you thinking, Momma Peach?" she asked.

Momma Peach turned away from the window. "I think I know where a deadly fox might be hiding. And if I'm right, then Mr. Floyd Garland will lose his job at the bank and also lose his wife."

"You mean you think Floyd Garland is being set up?"

"I think that ugly snake wanted Mr. Graystone dead, God rest his poor soul. But I also think he was just a pawn. We have more players on the board than we know about. I don't know about chess now, but I like to play Monopoly. Oh, I love to land on Boardwalk, too," Momma Peach chuckled. "But I ain't stupid. I know how to watch the other players and I know when to put motels on cheap property to wear down my opponents."

"Okay, Momma Peach," Michelle said with a grin, but she fought back a yawn as she said, "let's go to the bank."

Momma Peach walked over to Michelle and studied her exhausted eyes. "On second thought, I will go to the bank alone. You go home and get some sleep and come by the bakery after it closes."

"Are you sure?"

"Yes," Momma Peach assured Michelle. "Mr. Rich-Pants is on ice right now. But his wife and the man wearing the money cologne are still on the loose. If we're not careful, they might leave town. I have to lay down a few sticky-glue mouse traps. Now, go home and sleep."

"Okay, Momma Peach."

Momma Peach smiled and walked Michelle over to the

office door. "You sure showed that snake a thing or two, didn't you? The way you jumped up onto the table and kicked him in the face...I ain't ever seen anything like that before in all of my life."

Michelle blushed. She always felt slightly uncomfortable when someone complimented her martial arts skills. She often reacted before she even knew what had happened. "I guess I let my temper get the best of me."

"Remind me not to burn your supper tonight," Momma Peach chuckled again and hugged Michelle. "I'm going to walk down to the bank, and then go have lunch at the diner. And if Mrs. Edwards brings me a day-old biscuit again I might just use some Kung Fu on her. And don't think I don't know about Kung Fu. I have seen my share of Bruce Lee movies."

Michelle shook her head and imagined Momma Peach wearing a karate outfit, running around an exercise floor, executing high kicks and breaking boards with her fists. Momma Peach narrowed her eyes. "What's so funny?"

"Oh," Michelle said and giggled sweetly. "I was just thinking that Bruce Lee would have really loved you."

"I think so, too," Momma Peach said and tipped Michelle a wink.

After walking Michelle to her Oldsmobile, Momma Peach strolled down to a two-story brick building sitting by itself on a piece of property in the little downtown area. It had a neatly paved parking lot and colorful flower beds surrounded by bright green grass along the street side. Four tall, white marble columns graced the front porch of the building, and they loomed over the street as if to announce the money and power hidden within was inaccessible. Momma Peach didn't care much for the building or the people inside – the only person she liked was Mr. Finney, the bank president, who she knew to be a decent soul. The rest of the employees had often made her feel as if...well...as if they were somehow better than her. It was as if working at a bank automatically granted them distinct privileges and someone like her or the other lower-class workers were not deserving. But, Momma Peach reminded herself, walking through a parking lot filled with both vehicles both rich and humble, it was always best to not judge and seek the good in folk. "Give me strength," she begged and looked up at the pretty blue sky. "Oh, how I wish I were a bird that could fly far, far away into Your arms," she prayed.

Momma Peach stopped at the polished brass doors, steadied her mind, and walked into a large lobby that smelled of mint candy and the Pine Sol they used to polish the floors each night. Imported pink marble covered the lobby floor, which extended to walls that were painted in sedate tones of burgundy and green. But it wasn't grand or beautiful; it was intimidating and awful, like going to visit the emperor who wanted to cut off your head.

At the front of the lobby was a long, polished wooden counter with five teller stations where people could withdraw their hard-earned money or feed it into the mouth of the bank. To her left and right, down short hallways, Momma Peach knew were the office doors where some of the managers and other employees worked. And way above her head, the second floor of the bank looked down into the lobby over a wrought-iron railing. That was where she spotted the *Off Limits To The Public* sign that led to the area only for the most elite employees. "Ugly place," Momma Peach whispered. She moseyed up to the front counter and tossed a smile on her face. A woman by the name of Grace greeted her. "Why, hello, Momma Peach. How are you this morning?"

Momma Peach stared into a face that was lost behind the falsity of too much makeup. It wasn't that she didn't like Grace Medford. The woman, she guessed, was decent enough. It was just that Momma Peach didn't like the plastic smiles and the fake charm; she didn't like the ugly, dark pink blouse Grace was wearing either. And oh, don't get her started on the way the woman had her bleached-blond hair styled. "I'm fine," Momma Peach told Grace. "But, please, do something with your hair and that pink...baby, there are prettier shades of pink."

Grace's eyes went wide. She lifted her hands to her hair, her fingers practically covered with expensive rings. "You don't like my new hairstyle?" she asked in shock. "I've been receiving compliments all morning."

"Looks like a cow spit up its mouthful of hay on your head. I have to be honest."

Grace nearly broke down in tears. "Really?"

Momma Peach nodded. "I've known your folks since you were knee high to a toad frog. You come from a good family, Grace Medford. But this bank is polluting you. Go get your hair back the way it was."

"But...my boyfriend said my old hairstyle was boring."

"I bet my best peach bread that your boyfriend hasn't called you since he's seen your new hairstyle, has he?" Momma Peach asked.

"Why...no...he said he's been busy," Grace said. "Oh dear..." she said in a tormented voice.

"Busy my foot," Momma Peach fussed. "I don't like banks. I keep my money here because my accountant fusses at me if I don't. But I know what banks are and what they do to people."

A snotty-looking woman in her mid-fifties overheard Momma Peach and walked over to Grace. "Is there a problem here, Grace?"

"No, Jane, there's no problem," Grace replied, wiping away a tear hastily.

"Yes, there is a problem," Momma Peach said. "Grace

needs the rest of the morning off to go get her old hair back."

"I can wait until I get off at noon. I'm working a half-day today," Grace assured Momma Peach. The snotty woman gave Momma Peach a cold look and walked away. "Momma Peach, do you want to make a deposit or withdraw?"

"I want to talk to a loan officer," Momma Peach told Grace. "I want a man loan officer, you know the one I mean? I don't like fussing at a fellow lady over money."

Grace felt her hair again with a hand sadly. "Of course, Momma Peach. I'll go see if Mr. Connor is available."

Momma Peach reached out and patted Grace's hand. "I know you think working at this bank makes you special, but it don't. I know you're special, but I see this bank turning you into a plastic card that ain't worth much. Now, don't get at me for saying that, but I have to speak the truth."

A young, beautiful African American woman wearing a neat cream-colored suit walked up to Grace. She smiled at Momma Peach. "You tell her, Momma Peach. I put in my two-week notice four days ago. I'm tired of this place. I'm tired of being treated like dirt because I'm not a Certified Public Accountant yet. People in this bank don't seem to understand that college costs money and making money takes time."

"Amen," Momma Peach beamed. "You have a good mind, Amanda Johnson. I know your family. Good people. I ain't sure why your daddy let you work here, though."

"Money is tight," Amanda sighed and looked over at the snotty woman. "I better get back to work," she said and patted Grace on her shoulder. "Come to work with me at the factory. The pay is a little higher and we get better benefits."

"It's a shoe factory," Grace said embarrassed. "What will people think?"

"Who cares? It's still in the accounting department there. We're both taking CPA classes, so what does it matter if we work at a shoe factory until we reach our dream, girl? Any place is better than this tomb," Amanda said with a serious look and walked away.

Grace sighed. "I'll go get Mr. Connor," she told Momma Peach. "You can have a seat in the waiting area if you want."

"Okay," Momma Peach said and walked over to the group of plush green armchairs that surrounded a coffee table that probably cost more than her bakery. She sat down, placed her pocketbook in her lap, and watched Amanda take the place of a woman who stepped away from the drive-thru window. The snotty woman Momma Peach didn't like approached Amanda, whispered a few sour words and walked away. Amanda made an ugly face at her. The other woman at the drive-thru window smiled and hurried away. "Maybe all the people in this bank ain't bad," Momma Peach laughed.

A few minutes later a young, handsome man with short, bright blond hair walked up. "Momma Peach?" he asked politely and straightened out his navy blue tie beneath his deep gray suit jacket. "My name is Bob Connor. I'm the new loan officer here at the bank. Grace said you wanted to speak with me?"

Charm dripped off Bob Connor the way honey drips off a honeycomb. Momma Peach looked up into the man's eyes and nearly melted at their sparkling depths. Standing before her was one of the most handsome men she had ever seen in her life. "Yes, I want to talk about making a new loan," Momma Peach smiled up at Bob. As she smiled, she read his clever eyes. Behind the charm and the polish was something darker and more sinister, but he was practiced at hiding it very well. He fit right into this bank, thought Momma Peach as she stood up to shake his hand.

"We can speak in my office."

Bob led Momma Peach down a short hallway and into a fancy office decorated with paintings and furnishings designed to look antique. His large, glossy wooden desk sat in the middle of the office, with neatly stacked papers and files, a computer, and a phone; Momma Peach didn't spot any personal photos on the desk. "Please, sit down,"

Bob said and pointed to a plushly cushioned chair in front of his desk.

Momma Peach sat down. She watched Bob walk around his desk and plant his backside in an expensive-looking leather chair. "Nice office," Momma Peach commented.

Bob smiled. "We try to create a welcoming atmosphere for our customers," he explained. "Now," he said with a smile, "what kind of loan are you interested in taking out?"

Momma Peach spotted a crystal candy bowl sitting on the corner of the desk. She leaned forward and studied the contents. She spotted butterscotch and peppermint candies sitting inside the bowl. "May I?"

"Of course."

Momma Peach retrieved a peppermint and placed it into her mouth. "I want to talk about making a personal loan."

Bob reached out and lifted a tan folder off his desk. "I took the liberty of pulling your information," he told Momma Peach. "You're a valued customer. Your payment history is excellent and your credit score is exceptionally high. I don't see any problem with you securing a personal loan."

"That's good," Momma Peach smiled and took a deep breath. "Kinda stuffy in here."

"I'm sorry about that."

"It's okay," Momma Peach said and let out her breath. "I like open windows. I don't like central heat and air...unless it's hot outside," she added with a big laugh. She swung her pocketbook onto the desk as she laughed and the folders and papers scattered everywhere in a mess. "Oh, I am so clumsy."

"No...it's okay," Bob said, and scrambled to clean up the mess and reorganize the files and papers.

Momma Peach waited until Bob cleaned up the mess before she spoke. "I'm a clumsy clown sometimes. I'm so sorry."

"We all have our days," Bob tried to regain his smile as he tidied the papers.

"I know we do," Momma Peach chuckled and then drew in a second deep breath. "My, what a handsome cologne you have on. I noticed it earlier but it really seemed to come to life when you began picking up the mess I made."

"It was a gift," Bob said shortly, distracted as he restacked the files on his desk. "Now, let's talk about the loan."

"Before we do," Momma Peach told Bob, "I want to talk about Mr. Floyd Garland."

Bob stared across his desk at Momma Peach. "What about Mr. Garland?" he asked in a voice that might have sounded casual to a rookie but was clearly stained with worry to the ears of a pro like her.

"Mr. Garland came by my bakery last night and said I owed a lot of money in back payments for a business loan I thought I finished paying off a long time ago. If that's true, then I need to take out a personal loan to pay those back payments," Momma Peach said calmly to Bob as she chewed on her peppermint.

"He said that?" Bob asked, his face almost blank.

"He sure did," Momma Peach stated in a matter-of-fact voice. "Uh huh, Mr. Garland said I owed bunches of money in back payments. Something about how the loan I made for my bakery was marked with an interest rate that was far too low for me to have? Now, I ain't no banker like yourself, Mr. Connor, because I thought that I paid off my loan fair and square."

Bob settled back in his chair. "I'll look into the matter, of course," he said smoothly to Momma Peach and regarded her with false concern. "I can understand your worry."

"I was going to speak with Mr. Finney...Mr. Finney and I are good friends...but why worry him? I think Mr. Garland was full of hot air."

"Mr. Finney is a very busy man," Bob concurred. "Momma Peach, you have my word that I will look into this matter at once. Right now, Mr. Garland is taking a personal day and won't be back in the office until tomorrow. I'll speak with him first thing tomorrow morning and give you a call."

"I will reward you with one of my peach pies," Momma Peach smiled. She stood up, grabbed her pocketbook, took one last piece of peppermint, and walked over to the office door. "Call me at my bakery, okay?"

"Sure thing," Bob promised.

Momma Peach winked at Bob and left his office. As she did, she saw Felicia walk through the front doors of the bank. Momma Peach waved at her. "Hello there," she said and hurried up to Felicia.

Felicia stared at Momma Peach in shock. "Uh...hi," she said in a confused voice.

"My, look how lovely you look in that peach colored dress. Peach is one of my favorite colors," Momma Peach said in a honeyed voice to Felicia. "Are you here to see your husband?"

"Uh, yes," Felicia said. "Floyd and I are meeting for lunch."

But Momma Peach not only heard the lie, she saw Felicia throw a panicked glance down the hallway toward Bob's office. She turned just in time to see Bob stick his head out and then yank it back in. "Well, enjoy your lunch," Momma Peach told Felicia, "and tell your husband I said hi. How is he doing, anyway?"

"I...haven't seen him since this morning," Felicia replied, having trouble keeping her nerves from her voice. "But I'll tell him you said hello."

"You do that," Momma Peach said and left the bank. "You do that," she whispered to herself and ordered her short legs to get moving back to her bakery.

Felicia walked up to Grace. "I need to make a withdrawal," she told Grace in a sharp tone.

"Yes, ma'am," Grace told Felicia. "By the way, did you notice my new hair style?"

"It's fine...your hair looks fine," Felicia said impatiently. "I need to make a withdrawal of five thousand dollars. I'm in a hurry. Floyd and I...we have a lunch date," she lied.

"I understand," Grace said and tapped away at her keyboard rapidly. "You seem to be making a lot of withdrawals lately. I hope your sick cousin appreciates all you're doing for her."

"I'm sure she does," Felicia said and looked around. She spotted Bob step out of his office and peer across the lobby at her.

After Felicia finished her withdrawal, she left the bank and hurried over to her blue BMW. Before she could open the door, she saw a shadow reflected in the car window as someone appeared behind her. She turned around and saw Bob Connor staring at her. "My money?"

"I'll leave it where I always do," Felicia promised in a frightened voice.

"See to it that you do," Bob told Felicia in a cold tone that brooked no disagreement. "If you try and betray me, I will kill you."

Felicia stared into the handsome face that hid a murderous monster underneath. "I...I'll do whatever you tell me to do, Bob."

Bob leaned close to Felicia and put his lips to her left ear. "I control you," he whispered. "If you even think about running I'll track you down and make you suffer." And with those words, Bob turned and walked back into the bank, leaving Felicia standing alone, trembling violently.

CHAPTER FIVE

*M*andy watched Momma Peach hurry over to the phone sitting on the front counter. "Is everything okay, Momma Peach?" she asked.

"I have to make a call," Momma Peach told Mandy and set her pocketbook down. "How has business been?"

"We're nearly sold out of peach bread. Had a busy morning crowd about an hour ago. Mostly college students buying up picnic food," Mandy explained and then sighed. "You should have seen them, Momma Peach. They were laughing and teasing each other...joking around and talking about where they wanted to have their picnic. One guy kept teasing his girlfriend about finding a bear. She pinched his arm and made him swear he wouldn't go searching for a bear."

Momma Peach looked into Mandy's sad face. She put

down the phone. Murder case or no murder case, her baby came first. "I see," she said and looked around the front room. "Okay, pack up some food. We're going on a picnic."

"What?" Mandy asked in a shocked voice.

"I am going to go down to the diner and get us some food. You pack us some bread and a pie," Momma Peach smiled and gently touched Mandy's cheek. "Where were those college kids going on their picnic?"

"Up near High Ridge Falls, I think," Mandy told Momma Peach.

"Pretty place," Momma Peach said in a happy voice. "I think I'm in the mood to see the falls today."

"Oh, Momma Peach, really?" Mandy exclaimed happily. She ran out from behind the counter and hugged Momma Peach as tightly as she could. "Maybe we might see...I mean...bump into the college crowd that was in here earlier? There was a really cute guy...he kinda smiled at me."

Momma Peach smiled from ear to ear as she hugged Mandy. "Maybe," she said. "Now, you know I don't like to drive. You'll have to drive her old clunker up to the falls."

"I don't think a 1967 Beetle is a clunker," Mandy told Momma Peach. "My dad loves your car."

"I keep that car because it belonged to my husband," Momma Peach told Mandy and let go of her. "Okay, let me walk up to the diner and get us some food. We are going to do this picnic right, just you wait and see."

Mandy watched Momma Peach grab her pocketbook and hurry out of the bakery. She squeezed her hands together in excitement, looked around the bakery, and let out a happy laugh. "We're going on a picnic," she said and began running around the bakery trying to decide what delicious desserts to gather.

As Mandy worked on packing their picnic, Momma Peach strolled up the sidewalk of the cozy tree-lined street, where beds of vibrant, red, white, and yellow tulips nodded under the tall pine trees. She walked past the mix of quaint shops and greeted people in passing. For a few minutes, Momma Peach forgot all about the black widow sitting in its web at the bank. She drew in deep breaths of fresh air scented warmly with pine and tulip and found herself thinking about her husband.

"I had your clunker repaired, you old scoundrel," she whispered in a sad voice. "It's sitting in the back of my bakery. I guess the day will come when you'll show up and take me home in that old clunker. Nah, ain't no cars in Heaven. I'll just settle for a walk with you, one day. Forever." Momma Peach felt tears sting her eyes. She wiped at them before anyone could see. "I miss you,

James," she whispered. "Sometimes the nights get awfully lonely without you."

Felicia spotted Momma Peach walking up the sidewalk. She hesitated, then, very nervously, hurried up to Momma Peach. "Uh, hello," she said.

Momma Peach stopped walking. She turned her head and looked into a very nervous and scared face. "Hello," she said in a curious voice. "I expected you to be at lunch with Bob Connor. I know Floyd Garland is locked up down at the jail."

Felicia looked down at the white purse she was holding in her hands. "You knew I was lying?"

"I know a lot," Momma Peach informed Felicia. "I know that you knew your daddy was in town, too."

"Can we talk someplace private?" Felicia asked.

"My, your tone has sure changed since yesterday. Yesterday you were a different woman. I saw you at the jail. I watched my baby interrogate you. I saw you lie through your teeth, too," Momma Peach informed Felicia and pointed down at a pretty white tulip. "Aren't the tulips beautiful?"

"Huh?" Felicia asked and looked down at the tulips. "Yes, sure, the tulips are beautiful."

"Flowers are like the heart," Momma Peach told Felicia in a soft voice, "they grow into a beautiful dream. But if we don't keep the weeds away, then the weeds grow over the flowers' beauty. It's never too late to start yanking the weeds out of the flower garden."

"Yeah, sure," Felicia said and began looking around hastily, embarrassed. She spotted a few shoppers coming and going, minding their own business, enjoying the morning. "I can see this was a mistake. I have to be leaving."

"Running is more like it," Momma Peach said and looked up into Felicia's scared face. "You thought Bob Connor was mighty handsome and decided to have lunch with him. What would one little lunch hurt anyway? But then one lunch turned into two and then three and before you knew it, Bob wanted to get serious." Momma Peach narrowed her eyes. "You didn't want to jump into the deep end of the pool, though. You liked to play with Bob, accept his compliments, lie to your husband about your whereabouts, play a dangerous game." Momma Peach shook her head. "What you didn't know was that Bob Connor was manipulating you. You were nothing more than a pawn on the chessboard to him."

Felicia began backing away from Momma Peach with eyes wide. "You don't know what you're talking about."

"Bob Connor wants to be the main man down at the bank. Your husband was an obstacle. Poor Floyd Garland has to be eliminated. And you," Momma Peach pointed at Felicia, "were the means to carry out Bob's poisonous task. How? I ain't sure yet, but I will be in time."

"You're crazy."

"What I don't know is how poor Mr. Graystone, rest his soul, came into the picture. Maybe you called him because you needed his help? Maybe Mr. Floyd Garland called him? What I do know is that your daddy didn't want anyone knowing he was in town...he especially didn't want Bob Connor knowing he was in town, ain't that right?"

Felicia continued to back away from Momma Peach. "You don't know what you're talking about!"

"Betty Walker is dead," Momma Peach said in a low tone that sent chills through Felicia.

Felicia stopped backing away. "Dead?"

"That's right. Strangled," Momma Peach said, keeping her voice low. "Your husband claims she threatened to tell the police a lie if you two didn't pay up. Betty claims that your husband threatened her life and then paid her to leave town. Who to believe?"

"I... Betty is dead?"

"Yes," Momma Peach said. She stepped closer to Felicia. "You pretended not to know where your daddy was yesterday down at the police station. You lied. You knew where your daddy was staying and you know who killed him."

Felicia began shaking her head back and forth. "I don't know what you're talking about. I...have to leave now."

Momma Peach reached out and grabbed Felicia's right wrist with her left hand. "Your daddy is dead, girl. Doesn't that mean anything to you?"

"You have it all wrong," Felicia insisted. "You don't know what you're talking about. Now let me go!" Felicia yanked her wrist away from Momma Peach. "I love my husband. I never flirted with Bob Connor or had secret lunches with him. And if you weren't so blind, you old bat, you would look into my face and see the family resemblance that is the proof of that." Felicia turned and stormed off.

Momma Peach raised her left hand and began rubbing her chin. "Well I'll be, there is a family resemblance," she said as her mind began wondering in a different direction. "Could it be? I will surely find out."

Momma Peach continued on to the diner, ordered two fried chicken plates to go, tutted over the biscuits which she said were too dry, complained about the vegetable portions being too small (oh, give her strength) and demanded she pay only half price for the food. Mrs. Edwards, the proprietor, an elderly African American woman, raised her cane at Momma Peach and told her to pay full price or starve. The truth was everyone in town knew Mrs. Edwards's diner served the best food. Momma Peach just liked to fuss and make a scene because she was a tad bit jealous. "Full price for dry biscuits and burned chicken," Momma Peach griped as she reached into her pocketbook and pulled out her money.

Mrs. Edwards lowered her cane. "Your fussing gives me gas, Momma Peach," she said from her habitual spot on a stool behind the cash register, wearing her usual khaki dress with her usual dip of snuff in her mouth. "One of these days I'm going to whack some sense into that thick head of yours."

"You just try it and I'll wrap that cane of yours around your hard head," Momma Peach promised and slammed a twenty-dollar bill down onto a wooden counter covered with photos of loyal customers, coupons, menus, receipts and a plastic tip jar. "I must be insane to keep coming in here."

"You come here, you stubborn mule, because you know I cook the best food in town," Mrs. Edwards told Momma Peach and pointed her cane at the dining room filled with hungry customers sitting at round, wooden tables throughout the diner that was decorated with framed photos from old yearbooks from the town high school. The floor was an ancient green and white linoleum that was cracked in places, but the customers didn't seem to care. They all loved Mrs. Edwards and loved her food. "How many people are in your bakery right now?"

"I sold out of my famous peach bread yesterday," Momma Peach said proudly.

Mrs. Edwards chuckled to herself. Her false teeth nearly fell out of her mouth. "Your peach bread would make a mule stand up and hee-haw."

"Why you..." Momma Peach mumbled under her breath. "Listen, old lady, I make the best peach pie and peach bread east of the Mississippi. Folks come from all around to buy my bread—"

"Desperate folks," Mrs. Edwards interrupted Momma Peach. "The world is full of them. Now, look at my diner and you'll see some decent folk with clear minds that know where to find good food."

"Give me strength," Momma Peach prayed. She reached down and opened a white to-go box and snatched out a biscuit. To her disappointment, the biscuit wasn't as dry as she had made it out to be. She savored the bite for a moment. But still, she was at war. "These biscuits ain't fit for a hungry hound dog. And look at that chicken breast...burned to a crisp."

"Cooked well done," Mrs. Edwards corrected Momma Peach. "Raw meat can kill a person. I have my customers' health to think about. Better to be a little extra crispy than to be a whole lot dead."

"Give it up, Momma Peach," Wilma Lynn said.

Momma Peach looked to her left and saw a middle-aged woman with short red hair wiping her hands on a brown apron tied around her waist. "Never," she said with a scowl.

Wilma rolled her eyes. "You and Momma Edwards have been at war for years now and not one time have you ever won a single battle," she told Momma Peach and handed Mrs. Edwards a meal ticket. "Table four had three lunch specials and three sweet teas, Mrs. Edwards."

Mrs. Edwards set the meal ticket down. "Thank you, honey," she told Wilma. "Go see if Maye needs any help in the kitchen."

Wilma smiled and walked away. "Wonderful girl."

"She comes from good people," Momma Peach agreed. "Now listen, I ain't got time to argue over these rocks," she said and tossed the biscuit back down into the to-go box, "just ring me up and let me get out of here."

Mrs. Edwards stared at Momma Peach. "Rumor is there has been a murder in town," she said in an undertone and picked up Momma Peach's twenty-dollar bill. "You involved with a case again, Momma Peach?"

"I can't talk," Momma Peach replied in a similarly quiet voice. Sure, she and Mrs. Edwards fought over food, but at the end of the day they were still very close friends. "I will say this: we have a black widow in town."

"Oh?" Mrs. Edwards said with one eyebrow raised as she handed back the change to Momma Peach. "I rang you up half price, as usual," she winked at Momma Peach.

"I knew you would," Momma Peach winked back with a broad smile. "I'll sneak you over some bread later."

"Extra sweet, just the way I like it."

"You got it," Momma Peach promised and picked up two to-go boxes. "Momma Edwards?"

"Yes?"

"What's the best way to catch a spider?" Momma Peach asked.

"You can't catch a spider, honey. All you can do is stomp them to death," Mrs. Edwards answered in a serious voice. "You be careful now, and carry you a heavy brick."

"I'll be careful," Momma Peach said and walked outside into the bright daylight. The sunlight caressed her face with gentle, loving fingers. Momma Peach raised her face toward the sun, closed her eyes, and drew in a deep breath. "I am grateful for the life You give me," she prayed with a thankful heart. "Thank you, Lord...oh thank you."

Momma Peach kept her eyes closed and let the sunlight

wash all of her concerns and worries out of her mind. She focused on the love of God and let peace enter her heart. "Momma Peach?"

Momma Peach opened her eyes. She saw Mandy standing before her with a tall, stringy college kid with messy brown hair. The kid was wearing a thick pair of glasses and an orange polo shirt that was so bright it made him practically glow in the sunlight. "Hey," Momma Peach said, looking at Mandy with inquisitive eyes. She looked at the college kid and gave him a welcoming smile.

"Momma Peach, this is Ralph. He was with the group I told you about earlier."

Ralph smiled awkwardly. "It's nice to meet you." He ducked his head a little bit, as if he wasn't quite used to being so tall.

"Likewise," Momma Peach smiled up at Ralph. "I'm assuming you want to take my Mandy on a picnic?"

Ralph looked down at his white sneakers, shifted from one nervous foot to the next, and then said: "I wanted to ask Mandy to come on the picnic earlier, but I knew she couldn't leave work."

"Well, she can now," Momma Peach beamed. She handed Mandy the two to-go boxes in her hand. "Go have fun."

"But what about you?" Mandy asked in concern. "I thought you were coming on the picnic, Momma Peach?"

"I think that I might be a third wheel," Momma Peach said and winked at Mandy. "There will be other picnics."

Mandy blushed as if she understood Momma Peach's wink. "I'll be back in a few hours. I locked the bakery up and counted down my cash drawers and prepared my deposit and—"

"I hear you," Momma Peach promised Mandy, "and I'm sure grateful. I don't like to close down my bakery before the sun sets but today I have to make an exception. Now go, have fun. And you..." Momma Peach turned to Ralph. She reached out and straightened the collar on his orange shirt, "bring my baby back safe or I will hunt you down like a rabid dog, you hear?"

"Yes, ma'am," Ralph promised and hurried away with Mandy. Mandy looked over her shoulder and waved at Momma Peach. Momma Peach waved back and then looked around. She spotted a pay phone.

"I need to call myself a cab," Momma Peach said and walked over to the phone, inserted a quarter, and called the Bakersville Cab Company. It sounded quite grand, but it really just consisted of three cabs owned by old Mr. John Barley. Twenty minutes later Mr. Barley rolled up to Momma Peach driving a run-down 1978 green Cadillac Eldorado. "You ready?"

"Oh, give strength," Momma Peach begged and walked over to the old man who was smoking a thick cigar. "Mr. Barley, don't you ever comb your hair?" she said sternly.

Old Mr. Barley shook his head no. "Ain't got enough hair to comb."

Momma Peach studied the blue and red Hawaiian shirt Mr. Barley was wearing over a pair of brown polyester pants. She sighed. "Doesn't Mrs. Barley mind that you're wearing a shirt with cigar burns?"

Mr. Barley shook his head no again. "Mrs. Barley is off seeing that sister of hers in Mississippi. She's been gone for two weeks. I'm down to my last clean shirt, too."

"I will just have to come over and do a load of laundry."

Mr. Barley shook his head no for the third time. "Mrs. Barley thinks more of that sister of hers than me. Leave the laundry for her doing. That'll teach her to run off and leave me alone. Ain't nothing wrong with that sister of hers anyways...darn woman is a hypochondriac who thinks she needs a team of doctors surrounding her every time she farts the wrong way."

Momma Peach cackled. Old Mr. Barley was still feisty at the age of seventy-seven. "Okay," she said as she walked around to the passenger's side of the car and climbed in, "I will treat you to lunch after I finish with my business."

"Where to?" he asked. Momma Peach announced her

destination as she buckled up. His overgrown eyebrows shot up when he heard where she was going. "I want a steak dinner for driving you out to that snake pit," he said.

"I will cook you some homemade fried chicken, mashed potatoes, sweet peas, biscuits and okra and you'll be grateful, you old coot."

Mr. Barley got the Cadillac moving. "Better than canned beans. Darn beans been giving me awful gas." And right on cue, old Mr. Barley let out a loud fart.

"Oh, give me strength!" Momma Peach yelled and quickly rolled down the passenger side window and stuck her head out. A few people walking down the sidewalk just then spotted Momma Peach begging for fresh air and shrugged their shoulders.

Mr. Barley shrugged his shoulders. "Better out than in, Momma Peach," he said with a half-smile around his cigar. Momma Peach kept her head out of the window as the Cadillac drove through the pine trees and the blooming magnolias. In the distance, a pretty brown finch hopped onto the sidewalk, snatched up a breadcrumb, and flew away.

Betty Walker's cousin was not pleased to see Momma Peach walk into the grimy front lobby where he sat idly flipping through a newspaper. Momma Peach wasn't happy about walking into a lobby that resembled the rotted inside of a green bean that had been left sitting in the sun. Mark Thompson was seated on the ragged, stained brown couch by the front desk, smoking a cigarette as he read the daily newspaper. "What do you want?" he asked and slowly lowered the newspaper.

Momma Peach tightened the grip she had on her pocketbook. She was prepared to tangle with this filthy specimen for the second time, if need be. "I want some answers and you're going to give them to me, if you know what's good for you."

Mark looked up at Momma Peach and then did a double-take as he glanced at her pocketbook. His mind was far too sober to even entertain the thought of tangling with Momma Peach. Given the bruises he still had left over from last time, the woman would surely beat him into an early grave. Besides, he was waiting for the local health inspector to drop by and didn't want Momma Peach to mess up the one unstained shirt he had found in the back of his closet. But he wasn't going to get cornered into talking to her, either. "I don't have time for this. Get out of here before I call the cops."

Momma Peach leaned against the lobby door and shook her head. "I know you were paid off," she told Mark in a stern tone, "but not by the same man who paid Betty Walker to leave town. No sir. The man who paid you off is a black widow, Mr. Thompson."

"Get out of here, lady, before I throw you out!" Mark hissed at Momma Peach.

Momma Peach began swinging her pocketbook in the air. "Let's rumble, boy!"

Mark threw down the newspaper in his hand, jumped to his feet, and like the coward he was, ran to the front counter and dove over it, breaking the cigarette in his mouth as he did. "You're crazy, lady! I'm calling the cops."

"And when you do I'll be more than happy to tell them that Bob Connor paid you to kill Mr. Graystone, rest his poor soul," Momma Peach said. She stopped swinging her pocketbook and narrowed her eyes. "Isn't that right?"

"I didn't kill nobody," Mark insisted and threw down the broken cigarette in his hand. "Listen, lady, you have it all wrong. I never met this Mr. Graystone in my life before he showed up one day and rented a room. I thought maybe he was a drug dealer...or seeing someone on the side...who knows? It wasn't any of my business. He paid me cash for the room and that was good enough for me."

"That's not good enough for me," Momma Peach said with fire in her voice. "Mr. Graystone was found dead in his room, poisoned. Someone murdered that poor man and that someone was you." Momma Peach stepped forward and cast out a cleverly baited fish hook. "And if you didn't kill Mr. Graystone, surely those sleazy eyes of yours saw who did!"

Mark nodded. He swam out to the hook as quickly as he could and swallowed it. "Sure, yeah, I know...something."

"Why didn't you tell Detective Chan?"

Mark ran his hands through his hair. Momma Peach was backing him into a corner. He had to think. "Listen, lady, I have to watch out for number one, you know? I don't own the Ritz, here. I deal with some pretty tough people who will break my legs if I even look at them the wrong way."

"I'm gonna break your skull if you don't give me the answers I'm looking for. Tell me about Bob Connor and I'll see to it that Detective Chan knows you did your best. Or I can tell her that you wanted this to go the hard way..." Momma Peach warned Mark.

Mark threw his hands out in front of him. "Okay, okay...just cool down some, will you?" he begged.

"You have ten seconds to start talking or I'm coming over that counter after you."

Mark stepped backward and bumped up against a water stained wooden desk that needed to be thrown in the trash – a far cry from the desk sitting in Bob Connor's office. "Okay...okay...you want to know about Bob Connor, right?"

"Right."

Mark struggled to steady his nerves. "I don't know much

about the guy. One day he showed up, shoved a bunch of money in my hand, and told me to call him when I saw Mr. Graystone come back to his room."

"When was this?"

Mark swallowed. "The night...the night Mr. Graystone was killed."

"You slimy rat," Momma Peach growled.

"I know, I know," Mark declared in a guilty voice, "but I thought, you know, it was a drug deal or something. I didn't want to get messed up in whatever it was. So, when Bob Connor shoved one thousand dollars in my hand, I just took the money and did what he told me."

"Don't play the victim with me."

"I'm not," Mark pleaded and pointed around the lobby Momma Peach was standing in. "I'm not rich, lady. I've...dipped my hands in a few bad deals over the years...and got on the wrong side of some very bad dudes. I learned to do what I'm told, keep my mouth shut, and talk to no one."

Momma Peach studied Mark's scared face. The slimeball was actually telling the truth. "So you believed Bob Connor was a drug dealer?"

"Yeah...and whatever was going down between him and Mr. Graystone was none of my business," Mark insisted.

"What time did Bob Connor visit you?"

Mark ran his hands through his hair again. "About an hour before Mr. Graystone came back to his room...about nine thirty, I guess...could have been closer to ten. I don't know, I was pretty drunk at the time."

"What was Bob Connor driving?"

"I didn't see."

"Was anyone with him?" Momma Peach asked.

"No, he was alone."

Momma Peach nodded. "Did you see Bob Connor return to this rat heap after you called him?"

"Lady, I passed out about ten minutes after I called Bob Connor," Mark confessed. "I didn't see a thing. Betty woke me the following morning, scared out of her mind, crying hysterically. She found Mr. Graystone dead in his room." Mark shook his head. "I thought she was drunk and overreacting, you know...until I walked down to the room and saw the body myself. The guy was dead. He had been dead for a few hours, too. His body was...cold." Mark shuddered at the memory.

Momma Peach bit down on her lower lip. "Tell me about Betty Walker. What happened to her after you saw Mr. Graystone? Did she leave the motel? Hang around? What?"

"Betty hung around until the police showed up and then I lost track of her," Mark explained. "I told her to take the day off and I haven't seen her since. My guess is she split town. Betty never liked dealing with the cops. Can't say I blame her."

"Did you see anyone come by after the police left?"

Mark looked down at his sweaty hands. He grew silent. Momma Peach nodded. "Talk to me. Have an ounce of dignity."

Mark shook his head. "I saw Bob Connor ride through the parking lot...and later I saw this pretty girl ride through. I swear that's all I know."

"What was Bob Connor driving? Don't lie to me."

Mark sighed miserably. "A gray Mercedes Benz. The cute girl was driving a flashy BMW."

"Mr. Connor didn't stop to chat?"

Mark looked at Momma Peach nervously. "Well, he...stuffed another thousand dollars in my hand and told me to keep my mouth shut or die. But hey, lady, I'm not stupid. I ain't going to the can for murder, especially not for a lousy two grand. No way."

Momma Peach grew silent. When she did speak, her tone was calm and steady. "You and I didn't speak, is that clear? I didn't come by the rat heap today. I didn't talk to you and you didn't talk to me. But," Momma Peach patted her pocketbook, "this tape recorder I have hidden in my pocketbook will make the police mighty happy if you decide to tell anyone I stopped by for a visit."

Mark's eyes grew wide. "You taped us talking?"

"I ain't stupid," Momma Peach informed Mark as she walked away. "If you try and leave town the police will hunt you down. I want you to sit tight. I am going to need you to testify in court."

"In court?" Mark yelled. "No way."

"Either testify in court or go to prison."

Mark stared across the lobby at Momma Peach. "Okay, okay...I'll testify in court, lady."

Momma Peach opened the lobby door. "Sit tight and don't leave this dump until I call you, is that clear?"

"Yeah, I get it."

"I mean it. If you leave, the police will track you down, not to mention Bob Connor," Momma Peach warned.

"I get it, okay," Mark begged. "Now take a hike. The health inspector will be here any minute."

"Take a hike?" Momma Peach asked in a warning tone and patted her pocketbook. "I'm going to have to teach you some manners."

Old Mr. Barley heard a man hollering inside but didn't

pay it any mind. A few minutes later he saw Momma Peach walk out of the front lobby, straighten her hair, and then make her way back to the car. "Everything okay?" he asked Momma Peach.

"Easy peasy," Momma Peach smiled and buckled her seat belt. "Now, let's go have a bite to eat. And I swear, if you fart on Momma Peach again I'll beat you senseless."

Mr. Barley shoved the car into gear and eased off the brake. "Not my fault that canned beans give me gas," he muttered and drove away from the motel. Inside the lobby, Momma Peach had left Mark groaning and holding his sore shoulder behind the desk, but she knew he would never speak rudely to her again. In fact, she was pretty sure she had persuaded him that it was high time to sell his motel and move to a new town – after he testified in court against Bob Connor, of course. He wouldn't leave town without showing up at court. Momma Peach would surely hunt him down and feed him to a pit of hungry alligators – or worse.

Bob Connor closed his office door at the bank and pointed at a chair. "Sit down, Felicia," he said, "and tell me what's on your mind."

Felicia walked to the same chair Momma Peach had sat in. "Bob, if I give you some valuable information, will you let me go free?" She looked at him with wide eyes and tried to hide her wariness.

Bob sat down behind his desk, slowly folded his arms, and regarded Felicia with curiosity. "Information?"

"You have a very dangerous woman after you," Felicia confessed. "Her name is Momma Peach."

Bob nodded. "Tell me more."

CHAPTER SIX

$\mathcal{M}$ ichelle sipped on a cup of hot coffee. "You could have gotten hurt," she told Momma Peach from where she sat on the front counter of the bakery.

"I ain't afraid of rats," Momma Peach informed Michelle and walked over to the front display window. The sun was just beginning to set, casting long, tired shadows over the front street. The birds were settling down for a warm night. Overhead, the western sky was beginning to transform into a bright, beautiful pink fire. "I'm trying to work this case out in my mind." She gazed out at the sunset thinking back over everything that had happened.

"I don't like you going one-on-one with dangerous people," Michelle said in a worried voice. Even though she was showered and rested, her body still felt tired. Sure, she was wearing a fresh, white, dress that went well

153

with her leather jacket – and sure, she kinda felt pretty, but so what? It wasn't like she had a date waiting to compliment her. Instead, she was sitting in Momma Peach's bakery going over new pieces of evidence as another lonely night approached. "Mark Thompson could have had a gun behind the counter."

"Mark Thompson is a coward," Momma Peach assured Michelle. "You said the coroner called you at home?"

Michelle took another sip of coffee. "Yes," she told Momma Peach. "Mr. Graystone was poisoned with a specific type of poison that causes the heart to instantly stop beating. It's a poison that is very difficult to detect, but luckily, the coroner's office had their suspicions and ran a few extra tests. Whoever killed Mr. Graystone, whether it was Floyd Garland, Felicia Garland, or Bob Connor, it appears that the killer was attempting to make it appear that Mr. Graystone died of a heart attack."

"This poison, where can someone, say a normal John Doe, get their hands on it?" Momma Peach asked.

"Nowhere," Michelle replied and set down the cup of coffee in her hand. "The poison was homemade. Dr. Murray was able to identify agents in the poison that affect the heart. The killer obviously has knowledge of chemistry or hired someone to make the poison."

"Chemistry?" Momma Peach whispered to herself, remembering something Felicia Garland had told

Michelle during her interrogation interview. "Felicia said she failed chemistry." Momma Peach turned away from the front display window. "I need you to find out if Bob Connor went to high school with Felicia Garland."

"Sure," Michelle promised. "I have to admit, right now I don't have much on the guy. He's squeaky clean."

"No connection to either side of Felicia's family?"

"No, Momma Peach," Michelle replied in a frustrated voice. "I checked Nadine White's medical records. Her records only show her giving birth to one baby girl."

"Felicia."

"Yes," Michelle said and jumped down off the front counter. "You said Felicia told you that there was a family resemblance?"

"That's what the woman told me," Momma Peach said carefully, still thinking. "We gotta dig up some bones on Bob Connor. Right now, Mark Thompson's word is worth a whole lot of nothing in a court of law."

"I agree, Momma Peach," Michelle replied. She walked over to the window and looked out at the darkening sky. "It's so beautiful tonight, isn't it? It reminds me... I drove down to Savannah a few months ago and took a walk on River Street. It was cold, but...there was a feeling in the air...strange, captivating...almost like I could hear the voice of the past echoing among the people walking the streets. I felt romance and sadness, hope and fear, pain and happiness...all wrapped up into that one voice."

Momma Peach stood beside Michelle. "I love Savannah. That's where I met my husband."

"How did you meet your husband?" Michelle asked Momma Peach quietly. Never before had she asked Momma Peach about her husband because she knew how bad Momma Peach still hurt inside. Yet, as she stood staring out at the approaching night, standing beside Momma Peach in a bakery filled with delicious aromas, the time felt right.

"I was walking on Bay Street, getting ready to cross over to Lincoln Street and walk down to a park. I was just sixteen and, oh, baby, life was full of beauty on that lovely morning. It was mid-spring, the birds were chirping, the flowers were blooming, the parks were green...oh, the Good Lord's artwork was a sight to see." Momma Peach sighed. "Those were some good days."

"Momma Peach, you don't have to—"

"It's okay," Momma Peach patted Michelle's hand. She closed her eyes and saw a young, sweet, Momma Peach wearing a soft pink dress wandering across Bay Street. "I was out exploring, you see. My folks didn't live too far from the downtown district and it was always fun to take the walk." Momma Peach smiled. "We were poor and

Papa only had the one truck. Everybody walked everywhere, in those days."

Michelle gazed at Momma Peach's sweet face. "I bet it was beautiful."

"Oh, it was," Momma Peach promised. "On that morning...May the 19th...I was young, beautiful, and happy. I walked all the way down to Forsyth Park and planted myself on a park bench." Momma Peach smiled. "I remember seeing a little squirrel fussing with a nut and the birds singing loud and beautiful. Children were out playing...mommas were talking...youngsters were out messing around, much like I was doing."

"I went to Forsyth Park when I visited Savannah. Very beautiful."

"My favorite park," Momma Peach told Michelle. "It was in that park that I met my husband. That old scoundrel was working as a groundskeeper." Momma Peach touched her heart. "My husband was eighteen and was so proud to be working a man's job. He was so proud, as a matter of fact, that he decided to talk to a pretty young Momma Peach who was sitting alone watching a silly squirrel."

"Sounds very sweet."

"Oh, my husband was an old scoundrel," Momma Peach chuckled even though her heart was breaking. "He tried to charm me, but I knew his game. He pretended to be a big man even though he was just out changing trash cans," Momma Peach smiled, "but it was honest work."

"Everyone has to start at the bottom. I started off cleaning floors before becoming a cop."

"That's because you're humble," Momma Peach told Michelle in a proud voice. "My husband was humble, too. Oh, he tried to act big and proud at first, propping his boot up on the bench, acting like John Wayne trying to romance Maureen O'Hara...oh, I love me some John Wayne."

Michelle grinned. It was a well-known fact that Momma Peach was John Wayne's biggest fan. "I know, Momma Peach."

"I guess you do," Momma Peach chuckled again. "My future husband cooled his act when I called him on his game. Then the future Mr. Momma Peach just asked me to have lunch with him and I accepted." Momma Peach fought back a tear. "The day I turned eighteen I married my husband. One year later we moved to Bakersville. Three years later...my husband went to heaven."

Michelle saw a single tear fall from Momma Peach's eye. "You were young then. You could have remarried," she said and reached out to wipe the tear away.

"I know the love my husband took to heaven with him still belongs to me. I'm waiting to have that love given back to me...someday," Momma Peach tried to smile but couldn't. Instead, she let more tears fall from her eyes. "Tears cleanse the heart," she told Michelle. Michelle wiped every falling tear away gently. "My baby," Momma Peach patted Michelle's hand as she sighed and seemed to find peace. "I'm ready now. Let's focus on our case."

"We have three suspects and an anonymous caller," Michelle told Momma Peach. She walked over to the front counter, retrieved her coffee, and took a drink. "Detective Mayfield hasn't been able to dig up much on his end, either. Right now, we have a lot of corners to inspect."

"How is Floyd Garland holding up?"

"Angry," Michelle confessed. "But he's not going anywhere anytime soon."

"Exactly," Momma Peach said in a pleased voice. "With Mr. Garland behind bars, we can focus on Felicia and Bob."

"As a team," Michelle said in a quick voice. "Momma Peach, there's tough customers everywhere in this world. It's not safe to go off alone, okay? We work as a team."

Momma Peach didn't argue. She knew Michelle's demand was born out of love and nothing but love. "Okay, I won't go wandering off alone anymore. Especially after having to put up with Mr. Barley's gassy stomach. Oh, give me strength, baby, give me strength."

"Oh? Was it bad this time?"

"Like rotted sardines on a sun-scorched day," Momma Peach said in a scared voice.

The telephone rang before Michelle could reply. Momma Peach hurried over and answered the phone, expecting the caller to be Mandy. Mandy had promised to call Momma Peach and tell her about the picnic with Mr. Orange Shirt. "Hello, how was—"

"Back off or everyone you care about dies," a voice hissed through the phone.

Momma Peach waved Michelle over. "Cowards don't scare me."

"Nice little girl you have working in your bakery. It would be a shame if she were struck by a car," the voice continued to hiss through the phone.

Momma Peach felt anger erupt in her chest. She spoke before she could control her mouth: "Touch my baby and I'll skin you alive and feed you to a hungry alligator."

"I'd like to see you try. Do as I say. Back off or I will kill everyone you care about. Betty Walker thought she could escape and now she's dead. This is my first and last warning," the voice hissed and hung up on Momma Peach.

"Oh, give me strength," Momma Peach said in a shaky voice and called Mandy's home. Mandy picked up on the third ring. "Mandy...you're home," she said in a relieved voice.

"I just walked through the front door. Ralph and I were outside talking...oh, Momma Peach, he's so sweet and—"

"I'm sure he is," Momma Peach interrupted, "but you listen to me. Stay inside and don't leave your house, do you hear me?"

"Momma Peach, what's wrong?" Mandy asked in a scared voice.

"Michelle and I are on our way over to you. Now listen to me. I want you to call Rosa and tell her to drive down to the police station. Tell her to not argue with you and just do what I say, okay?"

"Yes, Momma Peach."

"Good," Momma Peach told Mandy. "I am on my way over to your house with Michelle. Tell your folks to be ready to drive you down to the police station. We'll follow you."

"Yes, Momma Peach," Mandy said, becoming really scared. "Momma Peach, what's going on? I've never heard you sound so worried before."

"Just do as I say," Momma Peach said firmly but lovingly and put the phone in her hand back down in the cradle. "If anything happens to my girls I will never forgive myself," she told Michelle.

"Did you recognize the voice on the phone?"

"No," Momma Peach answered honestly. "I know it was Bob Connor, though. Find out where that snake is."

Michelle nodded. She grabbed the phone and called the police station. "This is Detective Chan. I want to know the exact whereabouts of Bob Connor." Michelle issued Bob Connor's personal details to the cop she was speaking with. "Make it quick, Jake. I'll call you in twenty." Michelle put down the phone and looked at Momma Peach. "Ready?"

"Let's go," Momma Peach said and grabbed her pocketbook.

One hour later, Momma Peach walked Mandy and Rosa into Michelle's cramped office, along with Mandy's parents and Rosa's grandparents. All six people looked extremely worried and upset. Rosa reached out and took Mandy's hand. "I've never seen Momma Peach so worried," she whispered to Mandy.

"I know," Mandy agreed.

Momma Peach closed the office door. And with much sadness, she slowly began to explain about the horrible phone call she had received at her bakery. Mandy's parents looked at Momma Peach in shock. Rosa's grandparents pulled Rosa into their arms. "Now listen," Momma Peach said, forcing her voice to remain calm even though she was scared, "two people have been killed. So whoever made the threat has to be taken very seriously. I am mighty worried right now, so I want all of you to camp out at the police station for tonight and tomorrow you will leave town until I say the coast is clear."

Mandy's mother looked at her husband. "I think that's a good idea," she said in a nervous tone.

Momma Peach looked at Mandy's parents. Mandy's mother was a tall, thin woman with short black hair who was pushing fifty. But Momma Peach saw that despite all her disagreements with her daughter, the woman was a loving mother who just wanted her daughter to be happy – even though she pushed a little too hard. Mandy's father looked like a retired linebacker who could still knock the stuffing out of a bulldozer. But his worried face told Momma Peach that all he cared about was his daughter's safety. "We'll leave town and go stay with my brother and his family for a few days."

Rosa's grandparents looked at Momma Peach. "We don't have no family to go to and no money to leave with," her grandfather said in an upset voice.

Momma Peach looked into a pair of loving, gentle faces lined with years of backbreaking work. Her heart broke. "I kinda figured that," she told Rosa's grandparents in a caring voice. "Tomorrow Michelle is going to drive you to the bus station."

"I have a friend in Miami," Michelle explained. "I called her earlier. She would like if you stayed with her for a few days. Momma Peach and I will make sure you have enough money."

"It will be okay," Rosa promised her grandparents." These are good people. You can trust them." Rosa's grandparents looked at Momma Peach and their eyes told her they were almost too scared for their granddaughter to trust anyone – but if their granddaughter said to do it, they would.

Momma Peach folded her arms. "I am going to get to the bottom of this case," she promised. "Right now, I must be pushing the right buttons, otherwise whoever made the phone call wouldn't have bothered to look in my direction. But I ain't gonna tolerate anyone threatening my babies. No, sir."

Mandy's parents pulled Mandy close to them. "Momma Peach," Mandy's mother asked, "you've always been more of a family member than a friend. We don't hold you responsible for any of this. All we ask is that you know how grateful we are that Mandy has someone like you caring for her."

Momma Peach looked around the room, she looked into the faces of people she deeply loved and cared about, and then she walked over to the office window. "Gonna be a long night," she whispered and looked up at a night sky filled with bright, shiny stars.

For the rest of the night, Momma Peach spent her time with Michelle digging in, making numerous phone calls, waking up a lot of people, and gathering as much information as possible.

When morning came, Michelle had two cops escort Mandy and her parents out of town, and then she drove Rosa and her grandparents to the bus station with Momma Peach. At the bus station, Momma Peach placed a thick manila envelope containing over three thousand dollars into Rosa's hand and kissed her cheek. "You tell your grandparents that I love them."

Rosa peeked into the envelope and nearly began crying. She looked down at the dark green dress she had on and wondered why Momma Peach cared so much for a girl who wasn't very pretty. Momma Peach lifted Rosa's chin with her right hand. "Don't you go thinking those ugly thoughts, either," Momma Peach told her. "I see a beautiful woman standing before me."

Rosa reached out and hugged Momma Peach with all her might. "I love you, Momma Peach," she said and started to cry.

"I love you, too," Momma Peach promised Rosa. She heard a Greyhound bus arriving in the distance. "Bus is coming," she told Rosa. "Now listen, that fellow over there is an undercover cop. He's going to ride the bus all the way to Jacksonville and then get off."

Rosa glanced at a short, fat man wearing a tan shirt, standing off to the side smoking a cigarette. The man looked like a con man instead of a cop. "Okay, Momma Peach."

The Greyhound bus eased down the street and pulled into the bus station. Momma Peach helped Rosa and her grandparents board the bus and watched them until the bus pulled away from the curb. When the Greyhound bus was out of sight, she let her tears start falling. "My babies," she cried and threw her face into Michelle's shoulder. "He threatened my babies."

Michelle gently pulled Momma Peach into her arms. "Get ready to fight, Momma Peach," she whispered, "because this is war. We have a killer to catch. Our killer is lethal and deadly. We have to be careful in our fight and consider our next move very carefully."

Momma Peach wrapped her arms around Michelle. She loved Mandy and Rosa more than her heart could speak. And now her babies were forced to leave town. Anger boiled in her heart. "I'm gonna stomp this spider to death real hard," she promised Michelle. "Real hard until there's nothing left but a black spot on the ground, and then I'm gonna pour bleach on that black spot and scrub it clean."

Bob Connor didn't know that all the wrath of Momma Peach was about to descend on him, Momma Peach thought to herself as she and Michelle drove away. But before she made her way back to the bank, they drove into a fancy neighborhood lined with expensive two-story homes sitting on lush green lawns that no child was allowed to play on. "My," Momma Peach said, admiring the houses, "will you look at these places," she told Michelle and whistled. "Mini mansions filled with some rich folk."

"They don't impress me. They just look impersonal and cold," Michelle replied. "A home is meant to be filled with people who understand how to laugh and love. I would rather live in a shack with you than live in a mansion with a person like Felicia Garland, Momma Peach."

"Same here," Momma Peach told Michelle, but her eyes still shone as they soaked in the beauty of each home. "I would sure like to live in a mansion with you rather than a shack, though."

Michelle couldn't help but smile. "I guess that would be nice."

"I don't make enough at my bakery to buy a mansion. And I doubt your cop salary is enough to buy a month's worth of those awful donuts you like."

"Ain't that the truth," Michelle sighed and slowed down

in front of a two-story house that was brick on bottom and white wood siding on top. A beautiful wrap-around porch hugged the house, filled with patio furniture and plants. A long, gray stone walkway led up to the porch from the road, ending at white marble stairs connected to the porch. "It is nice," she said to Momma Peach. "This house belongs to Felicia Garland."

Momma Peach nodded. She spotted Felicia's BMW parked in a small concrete driveway on the side of the house, next to the two-car garage. Michelle pulled her Oldsmobile up behind the BMW and parked. As she did, Felicia Garland stepped outside through a door connected to the front of the garage and was startled to see them. "Unless you have a warrant, get off my property," she demanded.

Momma Peach climbed out of the Oldsmobile and looked at Felicia. She watched as a soft, warm, wind played with the folds of the long, gray dress Felicia wore. And for a second – a mere second in time – the woman actually appeared beautiful. "Where are you going, Mrs. Garland?" Michelle asked, slamming the driver's side door shut.

"Do you have a warrant?" Felicia asked suspiciously.

"No," Michelle said and turned to look at Momma Peach.

"Bob Connor threatened to kill my babies," Momma Peach told Felicia in a quietly serious tone that stopped

Felicia in her tracks. "Bob Connor didn't know who I was, did he? Maybe he had a scent of me, but nothing to really get his undergarments in a twist over. Someone talked to Bob Connor about me, someone," Momma Peach pointed a hard finger at Felicia, "who is trying to figure out what team she wants to play on."

"I don't know what you're talking about," Felicia told Momma Peach. She walked over to her BMW, fished out a set of car keys from the white purse she was holding and began unlocking the driver's side door. Momma Peach quickly walked over to the BMW and leaned against the driver's side door before Felicia could open it. "What do you think you're doing?"

"I was wrong in thinking you and Bob Connor were playing footsie under the table," Momma Peach told Felicia, still stubbornly pressing her body weight against the driver's side door, "but I can't find this so-called family resemblance either."

Felicia pulled futilely at the door handle and turned to look at the detective in outrage. But as she watched, Michelle nonchalantly leaned on the hood of the Oldsmobile and seemed perfectly comfortable letting her continue to struggle. "Get off my car," she demanded, turning furiously back to Momma Peach.

"Your mother's side of the family were all attorneys," Momma Peach replied, "isn't that neat. I mean, it's neat if you have something to hide." Momma Peach folded her arms together. "It's really neat if you had a baby that was, well, a little mistake, and you wanted to erase the birth of that baby off your medical records. I'm sure a family of attorneys could accomplish that task, right?"

"You're insane."

"Enough," Momma Peach snapped. "If you insist on acting like a stupid little brat any longer I'm going to beat you bowlegged with my bare hands. Your daddy is dead. Betty Walker is dead. My babies have been forced to leave town. I'm mighty mad right now and I want answers. Now tell me why you talked to Bob Connor? And don't say you didn't because I know you did. And it's because of your stupid, fat mouth that my babies' lives were put in danger. So you better speak to me and tell me the truth or I'm going to go to prison for killing you with my bare hands right here in this fancy driveway."

"Better talk to her," Michelle warned Felicia. "I can't make an official arrest until she attacks you."

Felicia looked into Momma Peach's angry face with true terror in her eyes, but she knew she was backed into a corner. "You don't understand."

"Try me."

"Bob Connor is untouchable. He's determined to ruin my life and threatened to kill my husband."

"Did he kill Mr. Graystone?" Momma Peach asked.

"I don't know," Felicia said, but immediately looked away, unable to meet Momma Peach's eyes.

"I see," Momma Peach said. The woman was lying through her teeth. "Bob Connor killed your daddy, didn't he?" she pressed hard.

"I...don't know."

"You're lying," Momma Peach snapped at Felicia. Before Felicia could react, Momma Peach reached out, grabbed her by the shoulders, and slammed her up against the driver's side door. "Talk to me before I put a hurting to you, girl."

"I don't know who killed my daddy," Felicia cried out, hoping her lie sounded authentic. "It's true, I knew my daddy was in town. I asked him to come to Bakersville to help me...kill...Bob Connor. Floyd was planning to hire a hit man...I begged him not to."

"Why?" Momma Peach demanded.

"You can't trust anyone," Felicia confessed. "I...my daddy...we..."

"Quit chewing your cud, girl, and spit it out!"

"My daddy and I were closer than I let on," Felicia confessed and broke down crying. "You don't understand...there are some dark secrets that are meant to be kept in the grave. My daddy...he came to Bakersville to help me end it once and for all."

"End what?" Momma Peach asked.

"I didn't want him to die, honest I didn't..." Felicia threw her hands up to her face and wept.

"Talk to me," Momma Peach told Felicia, lowering her tone.

Felicia kept her face hidden. "I did speak to Bob about you," Felicia confessed. "I told him that you were becoming a threat. I needed a way to get on his good side, to show him that I could be trusted...because...because..."

"You want to kill him too, right?" Momma Peach asked.

Felicia nodded her head. "Bob will go after Floyd next," she said in a terrified voice. "Floyd and I had to play dumb for the police and handle our affairs in the shadows. It's true, Floyd paid Betty Walker to leave town, but he didn't kill her. Betty...saw something she shouldn't have."

"What?" Momma Peach insisted.

Felicia finally removed her hands from her teary face and looked at Momma Peach. "It shouldn't have happened at all. What kind of crazy maid service brings towels to your room so early in the morning?" she asked Momma Peach in a desperate voice.

Momma Peach glanced at Michelle. "Go on."

Felicia looked up at a tall, gorgeous pine tree and closed her eyes. "Betty saw the killer."

"I see," Momma Peach said and took a deep breath. "Let's apply the brakes a second and go back to the night your daddy was killed. What was he doing in my bakery in the first place?"

"Waiting for me," Felicia confessed. "I met my daddy outside of your bakery and drove him back to that awful motel. We...knew Bob was watching me. We wanted...needed...him to see us together." Felicia forced her nerves to settle down. "Oh, it was such a mess."

"People make life messy with their lies," Momma Peach pointed out. "Now you just keep on talking."

"I've said too much already."

"You ain't said nothing yet," Momma Peach pressed Felicia with a hard look. "Your daddy killed your momma, didn't he? He wanted her money."

Felicia's eyes grew wide. "I...what are you...I mean, that's just crazy."

"You said your daddy flew them green helicopters in Vietnam but then ended up fixing toilets. That didn't make sense to me so I set my mind to thinking about that last night when I was resting in my favorite chair and soaking my poor feet." Momma Peach glanced at Michelle. Michelle was listening to her every word.

173

"Your momma, according to you, came from a rich family of lawyers."

"Yes."

"Your daddy wanted her money, but why would a rich woman like your momma marry a man who went from flying with the birds to fixing toilets?" Momma Peach leaned close to Felicia. "Not unless he had leverage. Your daddy had something on your momma, didn't he? We ran your daddy's military records. He was kicked out of the Army for flying drunk. Now, why would a rich woman marry a man who got booted out of the Army and had his pilot's license yanked out from under his feet?"

"I don't—" Felicia began to speak.

Momma Peach interrupted her. "I ran your momma's records," she told Felicia. "Your momma was born way up there in Brooklyn, New York. In her younger years, she dated a very dangerous man who was arrested by the FBI for murder." Momma Peach shook her head. "The man the FBI arrested was a hit man for the mafia, woman. He went around, uh, whacking people...did I say that right Michelle?"

"Yes, Momma Peach."

Momma Peach nodded. "And your daddy became a secret agent—"

"Informant," Michelle corrected Momma Peach.

"Thank you," Momma Peach said. "Your daddy became an informant for the FBI. Why? Because after he got kicked out of the Army, he went back to his home in Brooklyn and became a...what do you call those hideous creatures, Michelle...wise mouths...wise eggs..."

"Wise guys," Michelle said.

"Thank you," Momma Peach said and continued. "Your momma and daddy was married in Brooklyn and they were both placed in hiding by the FBI after they both testified in court and sent a very angry Mafia guy...a wise guy...whatever you call them...to prison." Momma Peach took a deep breath. "Bob Connor is the son of the hit man your momma helped send up the creek bed—"

"River, Momma Peach. Her momma sent Bob Connor's father up the river."

"Thank you, again." Momma Peach stared into Felicia's eyes. "Those little computer things are really neat. Too complicated for me to even think about understanding, but my baby standing over there is a genius. You should have seen her making that computer down at the police station talk. My, it was neat."

"Please—"

"Your momma's family wasn't too happy about her choices in men," Momma Peach continued. "My, she comes from a line of good folk. But, there's always a rotten egg in every carton." Momma Peach nodded. "Yes, ma'am, there sure is. But your momma cleaned up her act after you were born. FBI records show that she quit drinking, stopped smoking, and even went to law school. She reconciled with her family and started acting right. But your daddy, he didn't change for the better. He kept to drinking, causing fights, getting into trouble, got arrested a few times. Records show that she was preparing to finally file for divorce when she was killed." Momma Peach scratched her right ear. "Whether she was killed on purpose or by chance, I can't say? Maybe your daddy did send her out driving knowing the poor woman didn't need to be driving? I guess I will never have a direct answer to that question."

"My daddy...was planning to kill my mother," Felicia broke down, unable to stand the steady stream of truth Momma Peach was firing at her. "Oh, I hated them...I hated them both...I hated having to hide who I was...and I hated my mother acting so high and mighty all the time." Felicia squeezed her hands into two fists. "Who was she to tell me how to act, huh? She dated a killer for crying out loud. She had her fun." Felicia shook her head. "My mother would have divorced my daddy long ago, but he knew her little secret. He knew she had an illegitimate child and threatened to write a letter to the prison where Rich DeDonato is at if she didn't pay him lots of money. All those years...year after year growing up he blackmailed my mother...not that I cared...or maybe I did?"

"Keep going."

Felicia kicked the front tire of her BMW. "I hated my daddy for hurting my mother...I heard them arguing one night. I heard him tell her that if she stopped paying him that he would tell her secret. I was sixteen...I didn't know any better...I was so angry at both of my parents...so I wrote a letter to Rich DeDonato in order to get back at them."

"I see," Momma Peach said. "What happened?"

"Nothing," Felicia said in an amazed voice. "I thought it was better forgotten, or maybe my letter had gotten lost in the mail. I ended up graduating high school, married Floyd, moved here...and then, one day out of the blue, Bob Connor shows up at my front door. That's when the nightmare began. This was shortly after my mother was killed, too...maybe Bob had her killed somehow? I don't know, honestly, I don't."

"Bob came wanting revenge, right?" Momma Peach asked.

"Money," Felicia corrected Momma Peach. "Lots and lots of money. He also forced me to tell him where my daddy lived in Restford. Bob threatened to kill Floyd. What was I supposed to do? So I called my daddy and told him what was happening. Together we devised a plan to kill Bob. But it couldn't be connected back to me. So I had to make it seem like I hated my father when Detective

Chan was interrogating me. I figured if she caught me in a few lies I could claim I was just repeating what my daddy told me."

"You mean about your daddy leaving his money to a few gray-haired soldiers?"

Felicia nodded her head. "Yes. The truth is, I'm in his will."

"We would have found that out," Momma Peach informed Felicia, shaking her head sadly.

"I know." Felicia looked embarrassed at this.

"Oh, I see," Momma Peach said. "You planned to make it appear that your daddy left his money to the old soldiers and then act surprised when you found out he left you the money instead."

"Floyd and I agreed that it would be very smart to deflect suspicions away from us. I mean, my daddy is dead and I'm set to receive all of his money? Obviously, the police would come knocking. But we never planned on him dying," she said, and hid her face in her hands again.

Momma Peach shook her head. "Woman, I hate to burst your bubble, but your daddy drained his accounts. There's not one red cent left in his bank account."

"It's true," Michelle said. "I ran a check."

Felicia lowered her hands from her face, wiping away a

tear, and stared at Momma Peach in shock. "I knew he kept cash on him usually," she whispered, "but..."

"After your mother was killed, your daddy told the FBI to take a hike and willingly left the Witness Protection Program," Michelle told Felicia. "Rich DeDonato was put to death about the same time he told the FBI to pack their bags. That's when Bob Connor showed up at your door, too."

"I don't understand," Felicia said, confused.

"Your daddy, we believe," Momma Peach told Felicia, "was not truthful with you about more than just the state of his bank account. He contacted Bob Connor in order to have him begin squeezing money out of you." Momma Peach saw Felicia's pretty face transform in ugly agony as she comprehended the truth of her father's dirty scheme. "Felicia, Detective Chan found out that your daddy took a trip to Atlantic City shortly after your mother was killed and gambled away most of his money. He was arrested for hitting a card dealer and let loose on probation. You were his meal ticket. He just had to get someone else to put the pressure on you."

"No, that can't be," Felicia said in a broken voice, "he swore that he was leaving me all of his money. How could he... I... Floyd and I need that money."

Momma Peach paced herself. "Why? You have a lovely

home, a nice car, your husband works at the bank. Why?" She let the question hang there in the air like a ghost.

Felicia grew silent. She looked away from Momma Peach. Momma Peach wouldn't let her pace lose momentum, however. "You were planning to frame Bob Connor for your daddy's murder, weren't you? That's why you called your daddy for help and had him come to Bakersville."

"And your daddy was planning on killing Bob Connor in order to blackmail you for your husband's money," Michelle told Felicia, "just like he blackmailed your mother for all of those years. Your father's intention, it appears, was to force you into a corner, leaving you no choice but to try and kill Bob Connor. Either way, he had you in checkmate."

"Computers are neat little gadgets, but the human brain is the real thing," Momma Peach said and tapped the right side of her head. "Reasoning skills and critical thinking are your best friends."

"Okay, so you have some theories, prove them," Felicia said in a shaky voice as she tried to gather her strength. "Get away from my car. I'm leaving now."

"Wait a minute," Momma Peach said. "Even though I'd like to punch him square in the nose, I know you made the poison that killed your daddy." Felicia stopped in her tracks. "Rest his poor soul." Momma Peach shook her head sadly.

"Why?" Felicia asked. She turned to look at Momma Peach with brittle anger. "Daddy always taught me to look out for number one. He taught me how to use my charm and my smile to deceive people. Daddy could charm a snake out its hole if he wanted to. Should I really stand here so shocked that he was looking out for himself? He played me, too...that's all. And now he's dead. Good riddance."

"I wouldn't tell Bob Connor that," Michelle said, "because Bob Connor, it appears, played everyone. And he'll be back for you if he thinks otherwise."

"Yes ma'am," Momma Peach agreed. "So go on and run. I'm sure Bob Connor will catch up to you sooner or later. But before you take off out of here like a skunk on fire, tell me, why did you call Detective Chan and report Betty Walker's murder?"

Felicia stared at Momma Peach like the breath had been knocked out of her gut. There was no way she was going to outsmart the woman. Momma Peach possessed a mind that was special and brilliant – a mind that would always be one step ahead of her. Felicia said lamely, "I don't know what you're talking about." But she hung her head down and didn't make a move, as if finally broken by the events of the day.

"Well," Michelle said as she walked up to Felicia, "until we can untangle this knot, I'm placing you under arrest for conspiracy to commit murder, Felicia Garland. I believe your intention was to kill Mr. Graystone, and I believe you made the poison that was placed in the peach pie he ate, but I don't believe you placed the poison in the pie. Not only did we find not a single shred of DNA or fiber evidence linked to you in that motel room, but there's one more thing. You see, you wear a very distinct perfume. The smell of your perfume was nowhere in the motel room Mr. Graystone was found dead in."

Momma Peach shook her head at Felicia. "Such a shame," she told her in a sad voice. "You're so young and pretty, but so ugly on the inside. Such a shame." Momma Peach walked away without looking at any more of the fancy homes. The homes were ugly to her now.

$\mathcal{B}$ob Connor welcomed Momma Peach into his office and closed the door. "It's good to see you again," he said in a pleasant voice that was, as before, backed with a steely chill.

"Did you get a chance to look over my information?" Momma Peach asked and settled herself down in a chair. "Love those mints," she told Bob. "May I?"

"Of course," Bob said with a smile that didn't quite reach his eyes. He watched Momma Peach retrieve a mint from the crystal candy dish as he walked behind his desk and sat down. "I'm not certain what information Mr. Garland was looking at," he told Momma Peach, as his voice changed from friendly to professional, "but you're in the clear. There are no records indicating that the interest rate on your loan was assigned in error."

"Now, isn't that neat," Momma Peach smiled. She popped the peppermint into her mouth. "Well, now," she said and settled back in her chair, "I guess you and me got other business to talk about, then."

"Do we?" Bob said. He leaned back in his chair. He studied Momma Peach with curious and cautious eyes. "Do you want to talk about making a different type of loan?" His face was perfectly neutral, as if he knew perfectly well she was here to interfere in his business, but he was going to wait until she made a fuss before his poker face moved an inch.

"Nope, not a loan," Momma Peach said and bit the peppermint in her mouth in half, "I want to talk turkey...with a turkey." Momma Peach stopped smiling. "What do you know about a dead man in a motel room?" she asked.

"A dead man in a motel room?" Bob asked in polite confusion. "I'm not sure I know what you mean."

"I promise you Felicia Garland does," Momma Peach said. She looked him in the eyes without blinking. "And right now, that lost soul is down at the police station in handcuffs because she couldn't figure out how to make the lies coming from her mouth work right."

"I see," Bob said. He slowly folded his arms together across his chest. "Felicia Garland and I have a personal history," he said in a clear voice. "I'm her half-brother. Did you know that?"

Momma Peach stared across the desk and all she could see was the vicious cobra snake dancing back and forth in front of her eyes. "Yep," she said. "But that would be mighty hard to prove in a court of law, seeing how your momma's medical records have been wiped clean of you."

"True," Bob said and sighed. "I was an unwanted child. I'm not bitter, mind you. My mother did what she thought was best for her life." Bob eased a smile onto his face that might have looked half-pleasant from a distance. Up close, it was crooked in more ways than one. "I was adopted by a decent family. I was treated fairly and attended a nice college. I have nothing to complain about. It could have been worse."

"Mr. Graystone is dead. I say that's pretty bad." Momma Peach braced her mind for a mental battle. "Strange how you arrive in town and suddenly your half-sister's daddy is found poisoned. Strange how a certain Mark Thompson confessed to me that you paid him to keep his mouth shut, too. Detective Chan is out in the lobby and she's mighty interested in speaking to you."

"I did pay Mark Thompson to remain silent," Bob confessed in a casual voice. "But only to protect my half-sister. When I realized that she was planning to kill Mr. Graystone – which you know already, of course – I knew I had to act."

"So you did know the man?"

"Yes," Bob said and nodded his head. "I had to be careful, mind you."

"I understand."

"I'm sure you do," Bob told Momma Peach with a smoothness that made her soul shudder. "I tried to save Mr. Graystone. I arrived at his room far too late, however, on the night he was killed. I found him dead. What could I do?"

"Call the police."

"And be arrested under suspicion for his murder?" Bob asked and shook his head no. "Felicia is a very clever woman. I knew she wanted me to find Mr. Graystone dead."

"Why?"

"To frame me for murder, why else," Bob told Momma Peach. "You see, she wasn't very happy to see me arrive at her front door. She was even less happy to see me working at the same bank her husband was employed at. Paranoia took hold of her poor mind, I'm afraid, and caused her mental state to fall into a very dark pit." He almost looked sad as he said it.

"Felicia claims you threatened to kill her husband unless she began paying you large sums of money."

"She's a very clever liar," Bob told Momma Peach and leaned forward in his chair. "My half-sister is not mentally sound. I have many of our conversations caught on tape that any judge would find very interesting."

"Oh?"

"I assumed Felicia's poor mind would eventually crumble and she would run to the police with a stack of lies," Bob told Momma Peach. "I had to protect myself."

"Will you bring these tapes to the police?"

"No," Bob said and leaned back in his chair. "I don't think that will be necessary. I'm beginning a new life in this community. I have been hired into a position that allows me growth and opportunity." Bob shook his head. "And I thought I had family here...however, I was deeply wrong."

Momma Peach chewed on the peppermint in her mouth. The snake sitting across from her was playing it real smart. "I smelled your cologne in Mr. Graystone's room. You were in his room for quite a while that night."

"Of course I was," Bob said. "I tried to save his life the night he was murdered. I knew if I called the police I would fall into Felicia's devious trap, so I tried to save him. It was the only way to stop her." Bob planted his hands down onto his desk and leaned forward to look forcefully into Momma Peach's eyes. "She needed me as a scapegoat. And I know why she needed the money, too.

187

You see, her husband, Floyd Garland, owed a considerable amount of money to a certain man who liked to take bets. Mr. Garland, perhaps out of desperation or plain stupidity, began stealing money from the bank to pay off his debt."

"Did he?"

Bob nodded his head. "Yes. But he was taking it directly out of the bank vault – he had access due to his position. The procedures of the bank meant he had a short window of time to replace the money he stole from the vault. Money he didn't have. Unless, of course, he somehow came into a sudden cash flow."

"Mr. Graystone's money?"

"Yes," Bob said. "Mr. Graystone's wife left him quite a considerable amount of money. I guess me showing up was bad timing on my part but perfect for Felicia. She figured out a way to save her husband from prison, she just needed a convenient scapegoat to blame for the murder of her father. I was to be that scapegoat. She just didn't plan on me seeing through her stupid little ruse."

"I see," Momma Peach replied. "Bob Connor," she said in a careful tone, "wasn't your daddy a hit man for the Mafia?"

Momma Peach's words reached out across the desk and punched Bob in the face, but he barely showed it. He narrowed his eyes. His lips almost curled into a snarl before he controlled himself. "What about it?" he asked. "Rich DeDonato did his time and now he's dead. He's square with the house."

Momma Peach saw a killer peer out of Bob's eyes in that moment. She also saw a man who had slipped for one careless second from his comfortable perch as a banking executive and revealed himself as fluent in Mafia speak. "Rich DeDonato went to prison because Mr. Graystone testified against him. Mr. Graystone also married the woman carrying Rich DeDonato's baby...that baby was you."

"I was unaware," Bob said through gritted teeth, though Momma Peach could see the lie seeping through his every pore. "Perhaps I should hire a lawyer to conduct a very thorough search of my family records."

Momma Peach shook her head. "Rich DeDonato is dead," she said in a calm voice. "Better to talk to folk when they're breathing. But I'm sure you did talk to Rich DeDonato while he had air in his lungs. At least that's what the visitation records at the prison he was rotting in showed."

There was a thin, strained silence in Bob Connor's office. His eyes never left Momma Peach's for a second.

"Get out."

"You visited Rich DeDonato many times," Momma Peach continued. "Warden at the prison claims Rich was running inside work for some low-down, good-for-nothing Mafia family and you were the middle man. Nothing like a son working with his daddy and his daddy's old friends, is there. Really bonds them together."

"Get out!" Bob said and struck his desk with one white-knuckled fist.

Momma Peach smiled. "Before Rich DeDonato died he made you promise to kill Mr. Graystone in revenge, and to kill Felicia, the daughter your mother kept after she gave you up. At least," Momma Peach widened her smile, "that's what Rich DeDonato's cellmate claims he read in one of the letters Rich wrote you."

"Back down, woman," Bob hissed in a low breath.

Momma Peach stopped smiling. She leaned forward in her chair and went eye to eye with him. "You threatened my babies you filthy piece of sewer scum. No one threatens my babies, do you hear me? Now you listen real close because I ain't gonna repeat myself twice: I'm going to send your sorry butt to prison where you will die just like your daddy."

"Is that so?" Bob asked and slowly began to reach for the top drawer of the desk.

Momma Peach knew in an instant. She jumped to her feet and smacked Bob upside the head with her pocketbook before he could retrieve the gun that was surely hiding in that drawer. Bob's head snapped to the right and then popped forward toward the desk as he absorbed the blow, stunned. "This is personal," she said in a voice that would have made a grizzly bear run in fear. "But let's work it out. If you have the guts, meet me at the motel tonight at midnight. I'll be waiting."

Bob rubbed his face and shook his head to clear his sight. "You're dead," he whispered. "And don't think for a second I'll let those pretty little girls working in your lousy bakery escape."

"Tonight...midnight," Momma Peach promised Bob and spit the remains of the peppermint in her mouth on the floor at his feet in disdain. "By the way, I know you killed Betty Walker. Betty Walker saw who killed Mr. Graystone. A letter was found hidden in her suitcase." Momma Peach looked at Bob with disgust. "She stated that you were in the room when she arrived with the towels. She saw you pick a small lid up off the floor. You didn't see her because she hid behind the ice machine and waited until you left before she entered the room. That's when she found Mr. Graystone dead."

Bob stood up. "The words of a dead woman will not hold up in court," he promised Momma Peach and pointed at the office door. "And I'm not playing your games, woman. I'll deal with you on my own time."

"If you don't show up at the motel tonight at midnight,"

Momma Peach said and walked over to the office door, "the tape recorder I have in my pocketbook will go public."

She could see his jaw tighten from across the room. He made as if to step toward her and she neatly opened the office door so that anyone in the hallway outside would be able to hear everything. "Midnight, then," he promised Momma Peach, his eyes flickering to the open hallway and the threat of discovery lurking beyond if any employee happened to walk past at the wrong second.

"Come alone. Felicia will be there," Momma Peach told Bob in a pleasant voice. Then she continued in an undertone, "But before I leave, tell me, how did you get Mr. Graystone to eat my famous peach pie? What really happened in that awful room? Tell me or I'll take my tape recorder right down to the police station quicker than you can blink, boy."

Bob's eyes flicked over to his desk drawer one more time and she spoke again, before he could move. "Quicker than you can grab that gun and chase me, either. Don't think I can't outrun you, snake."

"Felicia and I worked out a plan," Bob said quietly, straining to look past her into the hallway in case someone was about to walk in. "It's true. I did show up and demand money from her. I hated her. I hated Graystone for ratting out my old man. I hated my mother for giving me up. My old man rotted in prison while they lived the good life. My old man wanted revenge, but the FBI hid Graystone and my mother." Bob pointed at Momma Peach and spoke in a fierce whisper. "You stand there acting as if I'm a rat, woman, while the real rats are running loose everywhere."

"Your daddy was a killer." She said this in a natural tone, as if she were inquiring about the weather. Anyone walking past would have nothing to suspect.

"My old man didn't kill anyone who didn't deserve it. He killed the worst mankind had to offer this world. The losers he whacked were nothing but guys who beat their wives, stole, killed, drank, ran drugs and guns, the works. Then it was their misfortune to get mixed up in the wrong family. My old man did society a favor." Bob's eyes gleamed for a moment with long-suppressed fury. "When Felicia wrote him a letter, she spilled the truth about my mother throwing me into the wind and that's when he got back into the game, from behind bars. My old man worked hard to find me. I was living in Brooklyn at the time."

"So Rich DeDonato found you, then what?"

Bob sat back down in his chair. "I went to the prison he was rotting in and paid him a visit. From there, things just sorta...went forward." Behind his quiet demeanor she could see the life of crime he had slowly but steadily hid behind the façade of his respectable work at the bank.

"But it wasn't until after Felicia's mother died that you were able to find Mr. Graystone?"

"The sap left the protection of the FBI," Bob said with disdain, but he still spoke in an undertone. "He got his hands on some serious cash after his wife died, ditched the FBI, and ran right back to his old stomping grounds in Atlantic City."

"Did you kill your momma?"

Bob shook his head no. "My mother was killed by a drunk driver, fair and square, no foul play on anyone's part...that was just really lucky for Graystone." Bob nearly spit. "Graystone was spotted in the casinos by a friend of mine. His wallet was picked and brought to me. I didn't want him dead, not then." Bob let out an angry breath. "I found Felicia's address in the rat's wallet and devised a little plan."

"So Felicia was the bait for your trap?"

"I targeted Felicia in order to draw Graystone to this little town in order to kill two rats with one stone."

"Felicia created the poison that killed Mr. Graystone, didn't she?"

"She's a very clever girl."

"But you were the one who forced Mr. Graystone to eat my peach pie. How?" Momma Peach asked.

"It's like I said," Bob grinned, "Graystone was a rat, but he wasn't stupid. He was working with Felicia, too, they were out to kill me. He knew I was out to kill him, too. So on the night he died I gave him a choice: eat the pie and die peaceful or die eating a bullet. No games, no theatrics, just two simple choices." Bob lost his grin. "Graystone had to die. He was planning to gun me down and blame it on Felicia! Of course, Felicia was unaware that her old man was playing her like a fiddle."

"Oh boy," Momma Peach said and wiped her forehead with her left hand, "the games people play. Families are supposed to love each other."

"Where was that love when my mother gave me up? In the Mafia, we were loyal the way my blood family had never been." Despite Bob's quiet voice, his face was twisted with vitriol. "So what if Felicia had her own agenda? I had mine. Graystone had his. I wanted revenge. Felicia wanted to protect her husband. And Graystone wanted money by blackmailing Felicia and Floyd for my death."

"Such a twisted little mess right here in my little town," Momma Peach said and shook her head. "Okay, now tell me about Betty Walker."

"The woman had to die," Bob Connor informed Momma Peach nonchalantly. "She was alley trash that could have cost me my freedom. I didn't realize she saw me until I talked with Mark Thompson. I realized that she must have seen me in the room searching for the cap to the bottle of poison I dropped. The cap had my fingerprints on it."

"I smelled your cologne in the room. But," Momma Peach pulled out a secret weapon. "I smelled a second cologne in the room, too. I wonder who that cologne belongs to? Maybe the person who called Detective Chan to report Betty Walker's death?" Momma Peach pointed at Bob's nose. "Snorting those drugs really messes with your sense of smell, doesn't it? You didn't notice the smell of cologne in the room when you returned back to fetch the cap, did you?"

Bob touched his nose and debated on whether to believe if Momma Peach was speaking the truth or setting a trap for him. "No one was in the room. I had the key."

"Oh, someone was in the room," Momma Peach promised. "You'll meet that person tonight. Don't be late now, you hear? And don't forget that I know you threatened my babies. Tonight, boy, you go down. I'm gonna stomp you into the ground so low you'll be feeling the feet of folk over in China." She didn't stay to hear his reply.

Momma Peach walked out to the front lobby. Michelle was standing near the front doors. "Everything okay?" she asked Momma Peach.

"We have a date with a snake at midnight," Momma

Peach told Michelle and looked over at the front counter. To her delight, she didn't see Amanda Johnson. She did spot the snotty woman giving her a cold look. Momma Peach waved at her. "Come by my bakery anytime for some of my famous peach pie," she called out and chuckled to herself. Having a sense of humor in a bad situation never hurt.

Momma Peach wanted to slap Felicia Garland clear across Michelle's office. "Listen you hardheaded dummy," she said in frustration, "we are offering you a way out. I know you called Michelle and reported Betty Walker's death. Why? Because you knew Bob Connor killed her and he was coming for you next. You were hoping mighty fierce that somehow the police would connect Betty's murder to Bob."

Felicia bit down on her right thumbnail, looking up at Momma Peach, who stood over her with a furrowed brow and her hands perched on her hips. She looked down again nervously. "Okay, yes, I called Detective Chan. I followed Floyd to the bus station...to protect him if Bob showed up. I spotted Bob's car, but he never bothered Floyd, thank goodness."

Michelle leaned against the far right wall. "You saw Bob Connor follow the bus, didn't you?"

"Floyd followed the bus...and yes, Bob followed close behind," Felicia admitted. She stood up from the chair she was sitting in and nervously began to pace in the small office. "Momma Peach, I'm already in so much trouble. This...mess...is so tangled. I admit I made the poison that killed my daddy...but I didn't kill him. You have to believe me."

"Bob Connor admitted to killing your daddy," Momma Peach told Felicia. "But you have to tell us what you saw."

Felicia sighed in relief to hear of Bob's admission. "Betty Walker saw him in the motel room...I was standing in the front lobby when she went to my daddy's room. Mark Thompson was passed out cold. I watched her ease the door open, stand still for a few seconds, and then run and hide behind the ice machine. A few minutes later, Bob came out of the room and walked behind the motel, where he had parked his car. I had my car parked in a driveway down the street from the motel."

"What about the night of the murder? Where were you?" Michelle asked.

"And who was really your target?" Momma Peach pressed. "You claim you and your daddy were working together to kill Bob, and maybe that's a half truth, but there's a few little holes, too."

Felicia walked to the office window, and looked up at a

dark sky blooming with rain clouds. She was in serious trouble. If she continued lying, Momma Peach would chew her alive. "My daddy was the target...Bob Connor killed him...and I...was going to blackmail Bob into leaving me and Floyd alone while...getting my daddy's money." Felicia sighed. "My daddy played me. I really thought I was in his will. I am his daughter for crying out loud."

"How were you going to blackmail Bob?" Momma Peach asked.

"On the night that I...found my daddy's body," Felicia said as she continued to stare up at the stormy night sky, "I called Bob first and ordered him to leave town or I would plant the lid of a vial that had his fingerprints on it in the room. Bob refused, so I went and planted the lid...then I called the police. I...oh, I was so stupid. I didn't think Bob had enough time to get to the motel and find the lid. I thought I was so smart. I wore cologne to cover up my perfume... Floyd would have been suspicious if he found me not wearing my favorite perfume...he wasn't aware of anything until I confessed the whole mess to him. That's when he got involved, went and found Betty Walker, and paid her to leave town...with the last of our money." Felicia hit her left thigh with her balled-up hand. "I was so sure the police would arrive before Bob could retrieve the cap. I was wrong."

Momma Peach walked up to Felicia. "I think we get the

picture," she said in a soft voice. "Felicia, let us help you. We believe that you didn't kill your daddy. But you're still in a world of trouble. If you do what we ask of you, we'll do whatever we can to help you."

Felicia looked into Momma Peach's eyes. "You don't understand... I'm not evil. My husband just made a mistake and gambled too much, that's all. He panicked and stole money that didn't belong to him. We all make mistakes. He planned to pay it all back." Felicia wiped at her tears. "When Bob showed up, my mind just...came up with this plan to save my husband, you know." Felicia laughed to herself. "Have Bob kill daddy, frame him for the murder, collect the money Floyd and I needed, and live happily ever after. It seemed so simple."

"Nothing is simple," Momma Peach told Felicia and heard thunder rumble in the distance. She checked the clock hanging on the left wall. "We have a few hours until midnight," she told Felicia, "so you better take those hours and decide how you want your future to be."

"I have no future," Felicia told Momma Peach and turned away from her. "Floyd is in real trouble. He's going to prison. I'm going to prison. Why would I want to risk my life tonight? Do you really think Bob is going to walk into a trap? He is clever...too clever."

"So am I," Momma Peach promised Felicia and put a hand on her right shoulder. Felicia pulled away, still looking out the window. "Let me help you," she pleaded.

"How?" Felicia asked. Her voice became angry and bitter. "Floyd and his stupid gambling!"

"Bob Connor would have shown up at your front door regardless of your husband's gambling problem," Michelle said. "Our problem right now is trapping the man. If you help us, I'll do everything in my power to help you, Mrs. Garland. Yes, you'll see prison time, and so will your husband. I spoke to Mr. Finney at the bank. He will be forced to press charges against your husband."

"No," Felicia cried.

"The question you have to ask yourself now is how much time you want to spend in prison?" Momma Peach said as a heavy rain finally exploded from the clouds looming in the dark, stormy sky and began soaking the earth. "Felicia Garland, girl, you better get your mind straight because as it stands, you are an accessory to murder and that's serious business. If you care about your husband—"

"Care about him?" Felicia spun around and glared at Momma Peach in agony. "I married him for his money...and then...I actually fell in love with him. How stupid of me, right? I actually started to love Floyd and stopped caring about his money. And now look at us, we're both destroyed...our lives are over. Nothing can fix that. So you can take Bob Connor and shove it, you nosy old bat. If you...oh," Felicia steamed. "Take a hike," she finished quietly.

"Is that really how you want this to end?" Momma Peach asked in a sad voice. She stared at Felicia with eyes filled with pity and sorrow. But Felicia's demeanor changed as swiftly as the lightning that struck outside.

"I wanted my daddy dead... I made the poison that killed him, I set him up... I drove him back to the motel the night he was killed...what difference does it make what my choices are now? My life is over, so take a walk off a tall cliff!" Felicia finished in a towering rage, her face contorted with pain as she yelled in Momma Peach's face.

Michelle walked over to Felicia before the woman had even finished catching her breath after this explosion and slapped a pair of handcuffs on her. "You made the wrong choice," she said.

Momma Peach looked Felicia in her troubled eyes. "Your soul is tied up in some serious knots, girl, but in time, if you have faith, you'll get them untied."

"Take a hike," Felicia repeated to Momma Peach in a sour, hopeless voice as tears streamed down her cheeks that her cuffed hands could not reach to wipe away. "I made my bed, now I'll lay in it."

"Yes, you will," Momma Peach agreed. She nodded her head at Michelle. "Take her away."

Michelle walked Felicia out of her office, leaving Momma Peach alone. Momma Peach stood in front of the office window and watched the heavy rainfall. A streak of bright, yellow lightning raced across the night sky again and vanished. Seconds later, thunder exploded and rattled the windowpanes of the office. "Let it rain," Momma Peach whispered. "Snakes don't like coming out in the rain."

A few minutes later, Michelle walked back into her office, closed the door, and made her way over to Momma Peach. "Bob Connor was at the bank when he called and made his threat," she told Momma Peach. "Right now, I have enough to make an arrest."

"He'll walk if you do," Momma Peach promised Michelle. "We have one thief and one deadly woman behind bars. Now let's go catch us a killer."

"How?" Michelle asked. "I agree with Felicia, Momma Peach. That man isn't going to walk into a trap and I'm not even sure what you're up to. How are you planning to take down Bob Connor tonight? And before you answer, I have to remind you," Michelle lowered her eyes in misery, "that my job is on the line, Momma Peach. I trust you...but if we fail to make an arrest tonight...let's just say this could backfire easily, and I know exactly how that will go. I'll get fired and never be allowed to work in law enforcement again. The mayor is already demanding answers and my boss is wanting an arrest made tonight."

"You'll have your arrest, I promise." Momma Peach

patted Michelle's hand. "Now listen to me, the snake we're after is going to have his fangs out tonight, filled with venom and ready to strike. He scared me something awful. His eyes are cold and soulless. And that's what I'm counting on."

Michelle looked up into Momma Peach's loving face that was filled with purpose. She saw a piece of her heart in Momma Peach's eyes. "I trust you, Momma Peach. Tell me what to do."

"That's my baby," Momma Peach smiled and pulled Michelle into her warm arms. "Oh Michelle, after this night is over you and me will take a ride down to Savannah and take a walk around Forsyth Park and then stroll down to River Street and get us an ice cream cone apiece and watch those big ships wander up and down the river. But right now, we have work to do, and—"

Before Momma Peach could finish her sentence, the door to Michelle's office opened and Mandy's beautiful eyes popped into view, her parents walking into the room determinedly at her side. "We decided that it wasn't right leaving you alone," Mandy's daddy told Momma Peach apologetically. Mandy ran over to Momma Peach and hugged her.

"I'd rather die than leave you," Mandy cried into Momma Peach's arms.

"Oh, Mandy," Momma Peach said as tears cascaded from

the younger woman's eyes. She wrapped her arms around Mandy. "You're soaking wet...you'll catch pneumonia! And is this a new dress you're wearing?"

"Daddy thought a new dress might cheer me up when we left town," Mandy sniffed and looked up into Momma Peach's eyes with a sad puppy face. "But I couldn't bear to stay away. I love you, Momma Peach. Whatever dangers there are, we'll face them together."

"Together," Rosa agreed.

Momma Peach looked up at the doorway and saw Rosa standing there with her grandparents. "We will not run scared," Rosa's grandmother said and made angry fists. "We will stand beside Momma Peach."

Rosa walked over to Momma Peach and hugged her so tight that Momma Peach nearly lost her breath. "We're a family," Rosa said and finally started crying. "I love you, Momma Peach."

"My babies," Momma Peach cried and pulled Mandy and Rosa into her arms. "Oh, my sweet babies are home with me." Momma Peach looked at Michelle. "Get over here."

Michelle walked over to Momma Peach. Momma Peach grabbed her and pulled her into the family hug. "My babies!"

Outside, the thunder rumbled and the dark rain

continued to fall. And meanwhile, across town, a figure in dark clothing stationed himself in the woods with a rifle in his hands, carefully training its sights on the Eagle Pine Motel. "Tonight, you die," the voice spoke in a vicious whisper. "Tonight, you die, Momma Peach."

CHAPTER EIGHT

*M*omma Peach drove her old convertible Volkswagen Beetle up to the front lobby of the filthy motel and parked. The rain was pouring down so hard from the sky that it pattered loudly on the closed roof of her car, and she wasn't sure how the car managed to even stay on the road – and her eyesight, oh give her strength, only by grace did she manage to see enough of the road to stay alive. "Testing, testing?" she spoke into the car, just loud enough to be heard over the raindrops.

"I hear you loud and clear," Michelle's voice came through a miniature two-way radio earpiece in Momma Peach's left ear. "I already parked. I'm working my way into the woods right now."

"Be careful."

"After I search the area I'll make my way to the motel," Michelle told Momma Peach. "Any sign of Bob Connor?"

She spotted a Mercedes Benz sitting in the rain-washed parking lot. "His car is parked in front of the room where Mr. Graystone was found dead," Momma Peach said, straining her eyes through the rain. "I'm going into the front lobby."

"Be careful."

Momma Peach turned off the car, reached into the passenger's seat, grabbed a blue umbrella, and climbed out into the rain. She looked around carefully as she opened the umbrella. The room Mr. Graystone died in was dark. Momma Peach nodded, bit down on her lower lip, and slowly walked up to the front lobby. The light of a single lamp was shining through the lobby's front window. Momma Peach approached the window and looked through. She shuddered, then looked closer. "Mark Thompson is lying on the floor in a puddle of blood," Momma Peach spoke in a low voice over the two-way. "I better check on him. Looks to be unconscious."

"I don't like this," Michelle replied over the radio as she maneuvered past one wet tree after another, searching the midnight terrain for any traps.

"I know," Momma Peach said, still quietly. "Let me play this game."

Momma Peach walked away from the window and

entered the lobby. The lobby smelled of liquor and cigarette smoke. "Mr. Thompson?" she called out. "Mr. Thompson, are you all right?"

Mark Thompson didn't move. Momma Peach closed her umbrella and leaned it against the front door. "Mr. Thompson," she said and eased closer. "It's Momma Peach, Mr. Thompson. Can you talk to me?" Mr. Thompson didn't respond, but she saw his chest rise and fall ever so slightly, and the twitch of his eyeballs behind his closed lids told her that he was fully aware that she was in the room.

Momma Peach bent down next to Mark's body and studied the pool of blood around his head. The blood was fake. She could smell the corn syrup in it from a mile away, even in the stink of that filthy motel lobby. But she knew to play the fool; at least for the time being. "Mr. Thompson?" she asked.

"Hello, Momma Peach," a voice spoke with deadly calm and perfect evil.

Momma Peach stood up. She saw Bob Connor stand up from behind the front counter wearing a black rain jacket and holding a camera. Bob grinned and began snapping photos of Momma Peach next to Mark's body. "Okay, that should do it," he said.

Mark looked up at Momma Peach, laughed, and struggled to his feet. As he laughed, the liquor on his breath was a foul stench in her nostrils. "You think you're so smart, don't you," he said in a hateful tone. The fake blood dripped stickily from his unwashed hair down to the collar of his shirt. "Well who just got played, huh? Tell me, you lousy cow. Who just got played?"

"You did," Momma Peach told Mark wearily and tossed a thumb at Bob Connor. "You think that snake is going to let you live? He's going to need a body to go with those photos he just took of us, you dumb donkey."

Mark's face went from spiteful to terrified in a split second. "Hey, wait a second," he said and looked at Bob, "you said if I helped you, you would pay me five thousand dollars and let me leave town in one piece."

Bob set down the camera on the front counter and pulled a gun out of the right pocket of his jacket. "I lied," he told Mark and coolly aimed the barrel at him, preparing to pull the trigger.

Momma Peach, against her better judgment, stepped in front of Mark in order to protect him. But this, too, was part of the game. "You already killed Mr. Graystone. Don't kill another man."

Bob searched Momma Peach's face. He then reached down and yanked a black walkie-talkie from a holster on his belt. "Any sign of the police?" he asked.

"She came in alone," a voice answered back roughly. "We're in the clear."

Bob put the radio back in the holster at his waist. "You actually came alone?" he asked curiously and then focused on Mark. "Down on the ground." Mark dropped down onto the filthy floor with a whimper and covered his head. "You're going to die tonight. But first I want to know what game you're playing. Why did you come here alone?"

"You killed Mr. Graystone," Momma Peach told Bob and then kicked at Mark's side. "Get up and be a man."

"You be a man," Mark cried out in a cowardly voice that was suddenly very sober.

Momma Peach rolled her eyes. "You knew this man killed Mr. Graystone and didn't do a thing about it."

"Leave me alone."

"Enough," Bob yelled and aimed his gun at Momma Peach. "Yes, I killed Graystone, and I'm going to kill you. But how you die is up to you. Slow and painful or quick and painless," Bob said and pulled a small, clear glass vial out of the left pocket of his jacket. "If you give me the answers I want, you will die a painless death."

"What answers?"

"What game are you playing?" Bob demanded again.

"You threatened my babies, and for that, your goose is now cooked," Momma Peach told Bob. "I came here to take the venom out of your fangs and you helped me do that in a matter of seconds, you pathetic dumb-dumb. But I ain't stupid. I know that when I see one snake, I better look for the nest to find its eggs."

"Oh, I see," Bob said. With skill and ease, he jumped up and slid over the counter and landed on the floor on agile legs that told Momma Peach the man was skilled in martial arts. "So, you figured out that I'm going to start running some of my pals from New York through your town on regular business trips, did you?"

"I figured that out. But first you had to take care of a little side business, ain't that right?"

Bob grinned. "Graystone is dead. My sister is behind bars with her husband. The bank is at my disposal. I'd say I fulfilled the promise I made to my old man. Now it's time to get down to business. This little town is perfect for running drugs and guns. And with my position at this little bank, I'm in the perfect place to launder the dirty money."

"I figured you were up to something. If you only wanted revenge you would have never gotten a job at the bank. There were plenty of other ways to get close to Felicia and Floyd."

"Aren't you clever. And it also occurred to me that you didn't record our conversation. If you had," Bob stopped grinning and hissed at Momma Peach, "I would be in handcuffs right now, wouldn't I."

"I figured you would come to that conclusion."

Bob stepped close to Momma Peach, keeping the gun in his right hand aimed at her chest. "What games are you playing, woman? I searched your records. You ain't with the FBI. You're just a small-town nobody who owns a stupid little bakery."

Momma Peach narrowed her eyes and looked Bob in his face. "I have my town to protect from you wise-mouth...wise shirts...wise...whatever you call yourselves. Now you tell me who the other snakes are and where they're at."

"You have a reputation for being a very clever woman," Bob told Momma Peach, shaking his head. "But right now, you're being pretty stupid."

"Listen, punk," Momma Peach snapped at Bob, "the police can take you down for murder, but that still leaves a trail of snake eggs in my town. I'm not even worried about you. I'm worried about who is going to take your place when you're locked up. Now I want names!"

Bob shook his head in mock wonder. "You're incredible," he told Momma Peach. "Do you really think you're going to walk out of here alive? Let alone with names?"

"Yep," Momma Peach said and touched her ear. "Michelle?"

"Loud and clear. I have the whole confession on tape," said Michelle as she walked into the lobby.

"Now, tell me the names I want and maybe I won't stomp you into the dirt so hard," Momma Peach told Bob with a look of satisfaction spreading over her face.

Bob's face drained of color as he looked from Michelle to Momma Peach. "You're dead," he hissed at her. "I'm no rat. You won't get a single name from me. And if you lock me up, you'll be dead before dawn."

"Road blocks are set up all over town," Momma Peach told Bob. "The State Patrol is securing all exits up and down the interstate. The only way you're getting out of here is on foot. You can kill me, but when you're caught, and you'll be caught for good, you'll fry for your crimes. Now tell me the names of the other snakes in my town!"

"Tell her," Mark begged from the floor. "Your plan didn't work, man. I told you this woman was dang smart. Did you listen to me? No—"

"Shut up!" Bob yelled at Mark. He stared at Momma Peach with venom in his eyes. The once-civil banker was gone and all she saw before her was the vicious criminal. He practically snarled, "I don't like losing."

"You are a loser," Momma Peach said and clasped her hands together. "Your kind are the true rats, boy. And my kind sets out the rat traps. Now give me some names."

"I saw a man in here tonight...he had a rifle with him," Mark said in a whimpering voice. "He's out hiding in the woods." Mark raised a finger and pointed at Bob. "That guy ordered a hit on you, Momma Peach. He was going to make it look like you were shot dead after killing me...a drug deal gone bad."

"I see," Momma Peach said. "Michelle, it seems we have a snake in the woods... Michelle? Michelle, did you hear me?"

But before she turned around, Michelle had already taken off, sprinting silently into the woods behind the motel. Over the miniature earpiece, Momma Peach heard the grunt of a large man hitting the ground and groaning in pain. The shooter didn't stand a chance. Momma Peach knew that all he saw before his life flashed before his eyes was Michelle's lethal kick and a disabling punch that tore into his body worse than hot bullets. And then Momma Peach heard the satisfying click of handcuffs cinching closed and Michelle's expert hands inspecting and disabling the shooter's rifle.

There was a small silence as Bob looked confused. "I've taken out the shooter," Michelle's voice finally came through in Momma Peach's ear.

"There's no more shooter. And you've got no more chances, boy." Momma Peach smiled sadly.

Bob gritted his teeth. He aimed his gun at Momma Peach. "You're still dead," he said.

The sound of approaching sirens floated into the lobby. Bob kept the gun trained on Momma Peach as he backed toward the side door of the motel lobby. "I'll be back for you," he promised with an evil grin and yanked the door open. As soon as he did so, he was met with a kick to the stomach. He flew backward into the lobby and as he fell, Momma Peach swung her purse into the hand Bob was using to hold his gun. The gun flew out of Bob's hand and crashed down onto the floor. Momma Peach quickly kicked the gun away. As soon as he recovered his breath, Bob yelled and shoved Momma Peach down onto the floor, trying to prevent her from reaching the gun. Outraged, he turned to run just in time to see Michelle kick the lobby door shut.

"You just made the worst mistake of your life," Michelle told Bob. She whipped off her wet leather jacket and dropped down into a fighting stance.

"You want a piece of me, cop?" Bob growled and matched Michelle's position. "I'll tear you limb from limb."

"Get him, Michelle," Momma Peach yelled out. She crawled up onto her knees. "Stomp that spider into the mud! Teach him to never threaten my babies again!"

Mark slowly began to crawl toward the gun laying on the floor. Momma Peach reached out and grabbed his legs.

"Sit still or I'll smack you into yesterday!" she warned Mark in an undertone. Mark hunkered back down.

"Where I come from, we don't pull our punches with nice little lady cops," Bob hissed at Michelle as they began circling each other in the lobby. Michelle remained deadly calm, her eyes never leaving his. Outside, three police cars raced into the parking lot and slid to a stop. She knew the first thing the cops saw would be the shooter, handcuffed and still unconscious. She had left him shoved up against the lobby wall nearest the woods, in plain sight.

"You pushed Momma Peach down. Now, you pay," Michelle told Bob.

"Die," Bob hissed and suddenly threw a flurry of quick, feinting punches, and then a vicious front kick toward Michelle. Michelle ignored his fake punches, and then spun to one side to block his kick so his foot merely glanced off the side of her body; she used her momentum to continue swinging around and followed through with a devastating roundhouse punch. Her fist caught Bob on the side of his face and nearly took him to his knees. He shook his head as if to clear his vision, and in a fury charged at Michelle and began throwing one hard punch after another with lightning-fast speed. Michelle blocked and dodged each punch with such skill and calm that he seemed to grow tired without even being able to touch her. Again, she waited for him to leave himself vulnerable, and then delivered a front kick to Bob's stomach followed up by a roundhouse kick with all the power in her compact fighter's body. Bob went flying across the lobby and landed on the floor. He stood up unsteadily, wiping a trail of blood from his nose and bellowed in rage. Again and again, he tried to charge at her, and she deftly avoided his blows, swept his legs out from under him, and delivered powerful blows that knocked the wind out of his lungs. Finally, he staggered to his feet as she advanced on him with a series of blows that he struggled to block, his face bloodied and streaked with sweat.

He collapsed to his knees. With the last of his strength, he stood up, yanked a switchblade knife from his pants pocket, and snapped it open. "Die, cop!"

"No thanks," Michelle said and crouched down again, barely winded. She grinned as he heaved and gulped air, attempting to recover. "Whenever you're ready."

Bob charged at Michelle with a murderous, desperate rage in his eyes. Michelle waited until the last, perfect second when he swung the knife in the air in a deadly arc. Then she launched forward, kicked the knife out of Bob's hand, and flipped her body over his in a powerfully elegant front flip. Before Bob could turn around, Michelle had him in a choke hold, her legs around his waist as her body weight dragged him down to the floor.

Bob pushed at Michelle's arms as she squeezed all but the smallest stream of air from his body.

"Nobody, and I mean nobody, pushes Momma Peach down," she whispered in Bob's ear. Bob struggled weakly to break free, but Michelle was too powerful for him and he succumbed. He felt handcuffs being fastened painfully tight around his wrists and moaned pathetically, as if he knew a life in prison was all that awaited him. The last thing he remembered was seeing Momma Peach standing over him and saying with satisfaction: "This is one spider we stomped real hard." And then...only darkness.

"Why didn't you tell me that you knew Bob Connor was going to run a crime ring through our town, Momma Peach?" Michelle asked. She took a bite of delicious peach bread and watched Momma Peach using a rolling pin to flatten out a ball of fresh dough. "I wish you would have told me."

"One step at a time," Momma Peach told Michelle as she hummed to herself. "My mind was full of some mean folks that needed to be taught a lesson. I knew that Bob Connor was bad news when I saw him working at the bank." Momma Peach smiled at Michelle. "You know, you look lovely in that white dress. White is your color.

And I love the way you're letting your hair flow freely today. So nice."

Michelle couldn't help but smile. "Thank you, Momma Peach, but please, don't try and change the subject. You should have told me."

Momma Peach continued to work on the dough with her rolling pin. The kitchen was hot and sweat was seeping out in beads on her forehead, but she was happy. Outside, the birds were singing, the sky was blue, and the honeysuckle bloomed full of life and fragrance. The air was warm and sweet and the pine trees tall and alive. "I learn to take one thought at a time. I knew when I saw Bob Connor working at the bank something was smelly. Bob Connor seemed like the type of snake that crawled in and out of many holes instead of just one."

"You mean running drugs and guns through our town and laundering money through the bank?" Michelle asked.

"Yes. Murder and revenge may have been his first objective, but he wasn't stupid," Momma Peach said. "Now, how is Momma Peach's famous peach bread?"

Michelle sighed and then smiled happily, popping another bite into her mouth and chewing it with a blissful look on her face. "The taste of this...the brown sugar with the peaches...it's almost as good as one of your hugs, Momma Peach."

"Thank you. And tell me, what's next on your mind?"

"Well," Michelle said and jumped down from the counter she was sitting on, "we have our arrests, we have Bob Connor on tape admitting he killed Mr. Graystone. Felicia and Floyd Garland are going to prison on different charges. Mark Thompson is having his motel demolished and the court ordered him sent to rehab and after that, strict probation. I would say all's well that ends well, except that your bread might be a bit *too* sweet today."

Momma Peach stopped rolling out the dough. Her face went from pleasant to serious. She narrowed her eyes at Michelle and shook the rolling pin in her hands at her. "What did you say about my bread?"

Michelle giggled. "Just teasing. The bread is perfect, Momma Peach, just like you."

Momma Peach winked at Michelle. "I know," she said and looked at the clock hanging on the wall. "I gave Mandy the day off. She has a hot date with Ralph. I swear that boy wears the ugliest shirts in the world. Yesterday he showed up at my bakery wearing a neon blue shirt...poor thing looked like a demented blueberry."

Michelle laughed. "I bet he did. But he's a nice kid. And Mandy seems to really like him."

Momma Peach went back to rolling out the dough. "What about you? Any hot dates lined up?" she asked in a careful voice.

Michelle took a bite of peach bread. "Detective Mayfield thinks I'm cute. Of course, he's sixty-five years old. I don't feel like dating a man who has to be in bed by nine," she sighed.

Momma Peach nodded. "I met a man at the grocery store yesterday," she ventured, "a Mr. Ryan Hillford. He's new in town...and he's single. No wife, girlfriend, fiancé, nothing. I talked to him and—"

"Oh, Momma Peach, you didn't—"

Momma Peach raised her hands at Michelle. "Before you use your Kung Fu on me, let me explain."

Michelle dropped her head forward. "To borrow your phrase, Momma Peach...give me strength."

Momma Peach chuckled. "Mr. Hillford is about your age and very handsome. He's opening up a paint and carpet store in Mrs. Call's old store. You know, the store that sits off by itself on Dove Street."

"Paint and carpet?" Michelle exclaimed. "Momma Peach, what's this guy supposed to do on a date? Bring me a bucket of paint instead of a rose? No offense Momma Peach, I like roses, not paint."

"Well...he seemed nice," Momma Peach fussed at Michelle. "My husband, my James, didn't work a fancy job, either. No shame in good, honest work. Good, honest work buys you flowers, not just paint. Now, I want you to at least meet this man. He's coming by the bakery around lunch to buy some bread, as it so happens. I told him you would be here and—" before Momma Peach could finish her sentence Michelle ran out of the back door faster than anything she had ever seen. "I'm going to have to work on that one," she sighed.

The phone rang in the front of the bakery. Momma Peach wiped her hands on the white apron tied around her waist and hurried to answer the phone thinking the caller might be Rosa. "Hello, Sweet Peach Bakery, this is Momma Peach speaking. Is that—"

"Who is this?" Aunt Rachel asked. "Is this Norma? Where have you been, Norma?"

"Oh, give me strength!" Momma Peach cried out in a whisper. "Aunt Rachel, it's me, your niece...Caroline! You called me. It's Caroline from Georgia!"

"I don't live in Georgia," Aunt Rachel answered in a confused voice. "Who is this? Where's my breakfast? Let me tell you about how late that breakfast has been lately..."

"Aunt Rachel," Momma Peach said in a louder voice, and then began to tiredly bang the phone against her head a little as her aunt went on and on. Just then, Rosa walked through the front door of the bakery, saw Momma Peach beating the phone against her head, and eased up to the counter.

"Aunt Rachel?" Rosa whispered.

"Yes," Momma Peach exclaimed in frustration and turned to look at Rosa. "Nice dress, Rosa. Love the pink," she said and continued to listen absently to the cranky tirade coming through the phone. Finally, she sighed. "Aunt Rachel, this is Caroline. You called me."

"Carolina? I live in Virginia, not North Carolina," Aunt Rachel said. Even from miles away Momma Peach could hear the woman cackle under her breath, no doubt grinning from ear to ear as she sat in her wheelchair stirring up trouble. "Where's my breakfast? And who are you?"

Momma Peach pursed her lips in frustration. "It's Caroline, your niece!"

"Knees? Knees don't trouble me. But I've got gas," Aunt Rachel announced. "Beans give me gas, you know. Don't serve me beans for breakfast. I'll sue you if you do."

"How can I serve you beans for breakfast when I'm hundreds of miles away?" Momma Peach practically yelled into the phone. "Aunt Rachel, did you get the replacement check I sent you?"

"Check? Oh yes, the nurses check my blood pressure every day. Who is this? Why are you talking to me?" Aunt Rachel asked with another cackle. "Maybe you ought to check my gas instead? I get lots of gas, you know."

Momma Peach handed the phone to Rosa. "Take this phone. I'm going to take a little trip and smack an old woman," she said in a strained voice. But then, suddenly, she turned as she caught a buzzing sound near the window. She craned her head forward, spotted a fly on the front display window, and yelled out, "Aha!"

Rosa stepped back with the phone in her hand and watched as Momma Peach snatched up a newspaper, rolled it up, and began creeping across the floor like a soldier preparing to ambush her enemy. The fly sat on the front window as if wondering what the crazy lady with the newspaper was up to. As soon as Momma Peach got close enough, she attacked. "Die, fly!" she yelled and began swatting at the fly as fast as her arms would allow. The fly took to flight and landed on a faraway shelf. "Oh, you think you can escape me, don't you," Momma Peach whispered and began creeping across the floor.

"Momma Peach will call you back, Aunt Rachel. She's busy right now," Rosa spoke into the phone in a sweet voice and hung up. Mandy walked into the bakery just in time to see Momma Peach launch a second attack. She walked over to Rosa, leaned against the front counter, and watched Momma Peach chase the fly around. "It's nice to have things back to normal," she told Rosa. "Nice dress."

"Nice top," Rosa complimented the blue blouse Mandy was wearing. "I know just the eye shadow you need to match it… I'll get it out of my purse. You keep an eye on Momma Peach."

Mandy smiled. She watched Momma Peach go after the fly with fiery eyes. "Come to me, I won't hurt you…much…now stop being stubborn and stay still…oh, you know you want to say hey to Momma Peach…"

Mandy smiled. Momma Peach was brilliant, amazing, loving and brave – yet the poor woman could not manage to catch a single fly. "Momma Peach?"

"Not now!" Momma Peach yelled as sweat trickled down her face, "I'm on a mission! I'm searching for a clever, stinky little fly that has a date with this here newspaper in my hand. Oh yes, that fly is gonna read the headlines up close and personal!"

Mandy wanted to tell Momma Peach that the fly had meanwhile landed on her shoulder, but she didn't have the heart. Instead, she looked at Momma Peach with loving eyes and smiled. For the time being, everything was right with the world.

But the idyllic peace and comfort in Momma Peach's bakery would not last forever. It would not be four hours later when Michelle would return to the bakery with a serious look on her beautiful face and urgent news for Georgia's most famous baker and amateur detective.

MOMMA'S RECIPE

UPSIDE DOWN PEACH CAKE

Ingredients

3/4 cup butter, softened

1/2 cup brown sugar

3 Fresh sliced peaches

3/4 cup white sugar

1 egg

1 tsp vanilla

1 1/4 cups flour

1 1/4 teaspoons baking powder

1/4 teaspoon salt

1/2 cup 1% milk

Directions

Melt 1/4 of the butter and pour into a cake pan. Sprinkle with the brown sugar and arrange peaches flat in the brown sugar.

In a separate bowl, mix the white sugar and remaining butter until fluffy. Add in egg, vanilla, flour, baking powder, salt and milk. When well mixed, pour over peaches. Bake at 350 degrees for 50 minutes.

Let cake cool and flip in pan onto a cooling rack. Serve immediately.

ABOUT THE AUTHOR

Wendy Meadows is an emerging author of cozy mysteries. She lives in "The Granite State" with her husband, two sons, two cats and lovable Labradoodle.

When she isn't working on her stories she likes to tend to her flower garden, relax with adult coloring and play video games with her family.

Get in Touch with Wendy

www.wendymeadows.com
wendy@wendymeadows.com

ALSO BY WENDY MEADOWS

MAPLE HILLS COZY SERIES

Raspberry Truffle Murder

Peppermint Chocolate Murder

Blueberry Truffle Murder

Sea Salt Caramel Murder

Georgia Peach Truffle Murder

Gold Flake Chocolate Murder

Coconut Chocolate Murder

Turkey Truffle Murder

Christmas Chocolate Murder

NETHER EDGE COZY SERIES

Murder & Spice

Where Pigs Fly

Ink-Slinger Murder

Made in the USA
Las Vegas, NV
16 January 2021

16067705R00134